US

Also by Wayne Karlin

Lost Armies
Crossover
The Extras

HENRY HOLT AND COMPANY
NEW YORK

Henry Holt and Company, Inc.
Publishers since 1866
115 West 18th Street
New York, New York 10011

Henry Holt ® is a registered
trademark of Henry Holt and Company, Inc.

Published in Canada by Fitzhenry & Whiteside Ltd.,
91 Granton Drive, Richmond Hill, Ontario L4B 2N5.

Library of Congress Cataloging-in-Publication Data
Karlin, Wayne.
US : a novel / Wayne Karlin.—1st ed.
p. cm.
I. Title
PS3561.A625U8 1993 92-6052
813'.54—dc20 CIP
ISBN 0-8050-1083-1

First Edition—1993

Designed by Katy Riegel

Printed in the United States of America.
All first editions are printed on acid-free paper.∞

1 3 5 7 9 10 8 6 4 2

FOR OHNMAR

With thanks to the Maryland State Arts Council
for its support, and to Amy Hertz for her suggestions

But [the pwe*] is, at the same time, a great deal more than a dramatic performance. Onto the theme of a religious drama, or a romantically fantastic tale of kings, queens, princes and princesses, are added scenes of the present day, or out of the contemporary cinema, clowning and buffoonery of a high order, wisecracks (often at the expense of authority), miming and mimicry (often of the hero and heroine or of persons in the audience), singing and dancing by those on stage, and the music of the orchestra. Here is something essentially Burmese, romantic, humorous, irreverent, enormously vital.*

—*F. S. V. Donnison,* Burma

By God, we've kicked the Vietnam syndrome once and for all.

—*George Bush*

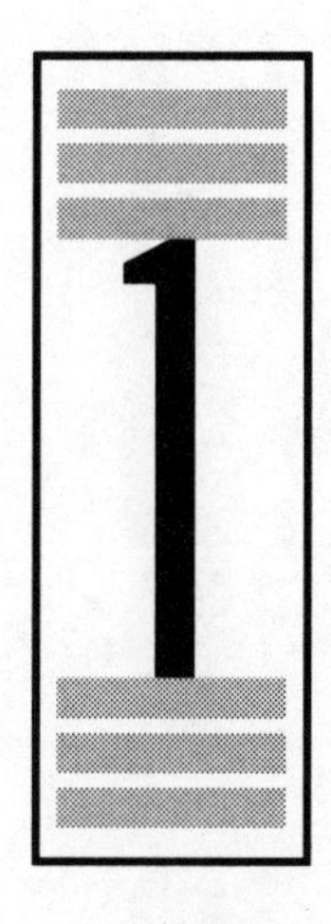

YEIN PWE

Nats are mischievous spirits who live in the jungles and mountains of Burma, dwelling in rocks or mountains or trees, in fields, in village or city gates, sometimes even in rain. Like the phis of Thailand, these prankster spirits will do much harm to the order of the world unless appeased with money, food, and the respect of belief. Of all the systems of belief in the world, perhaps a faith in mischief is the most realistic.

A Burmese king, Anawrahta, tried to stop the worship of nats when he brought Theravada Buddhism to Upper Burma. Like all kings, jailers, and barkeeps, Anawrahta wanted to fit his unruly people into his idea of what they should be; he thought of nats as dreams of disorder and disruption freed into the world. So the king brought in his own nat, Thagyamin, and declared him ruler of the thirty-six greatest nats of Burma, and since he was the king, everybody had to believe him. Thus from an anarchy of spirits, a hierarchy was formed in the hearts and minds of the people, with Anawrahta's nat at its peak. The uniformity for which he hungered was achieved. Anawrahta became the king of the day and the king of dreams. There were no exits from his vision. Everybody fit in the program.

But nats will still be nats.

▪ ▪ ▪

A nat was sitting with Fat Al, Chuckie's-in-Love, and Helicopter Harry. Tall, thin, stubble-bearded, filthy hair wild and spiked as elephant grass. The left side of his neck bumped and cracked with scar tissue. Montagnard bracelets dangling from sticklike wrists. He grinned, exposing worn brown-and-yellow nubs of teeth.

Loman looked away from him, around the bar.

His customers looked like all thirty-seven nats.

Or maybe it was all that red light. The Naga Queen was lit like an oven. Loman had had the walls and ceiling cushioned with rolls of black Naugahyde, so that being inside was like being entombed in a Tijuana upholstery job. The glasses hanging from the bamboo rack over the bar gleamed with ruby stars, and the wall-to-wall mirror behind it presented the customers with their own fire-licked faces as well as the sweaty back of the adolescent girl dancing nude on the bar. The amber light and black shadows cast the drinkers as leering carvings on a temple wall in some ruin of a jungle city. In the smudged, slightly distorting glass of the mirror, Loman could see each group of demons in its appointed place: Singapore Chinese, Japanese, and Germans on sex tours, the American vets who made the Naga Queen their home.

"There's some people I want you to meet," Jimmy Chang said. "Tomorrow." He looked at the tight, sweat-streaked behind in front of him and raised his glass. The beer shifted in it, its froth red-tinted.

"Who?"

"This strange couple. Like us, man."

Loman regarded himself and Jimmy in the mirror, sitting side by side, a slim, pock-faced Chinese next to a big, middle-aged white man with cropped black hair and a barroom spread. Jimmy grinned at him.

"What's lub got to do wid it?" the Filipina singer asked. In the reverse world of the mirror, Loman watched the German tourists who were being fondled for drinks by the bar girls sitting like painted children in their laps. Some of the men were twisting the girls' breasts.

He saw Jimmy, in the mirror, looking at him looking at them. Jimmy must have seen something in his face; he put a hand on Loman's arm.

"Being a daddy is bad for business. Girls just want to have fun, man."

The Filipina singer echoed him unconvincingly.

She stopped and began singing a Thai song that had become popular over the last few months, a ballad about Taksin, one of the northern rebel leaders. Loman saw the other girls cease their fondling for a second, turn to listen. He waved at the girl and she stopped, went back to American music.

The girl dancing on the bar came in front of him, trying to catch his eye, thrusting the small, black comma of her loins toward him. It was considered good fortune to work for the *farang*: his girls got individual cubicles instead of being packed four to six into a five-by-eight space; they could decorate the walls with all the movie and rock-star posters they wanted; they weren't beaten and they weren't kept in constant debt for clothing and food. They had money they could send back to the parents in the Triangle who had sold them down to Bangkok. A number of them had become second wives to Thai customers or first wives to the American veterans. Two girls even had opened their own bars, where they maximized profit by making their girls sleep packed together in tiny cubicles. But Loman didn't do that. He cut down on his profit and lived with himself. He was a good and fair pimp.

He toasted the mirror.

There was a rise in the voices from the vets' table that made Loman and Jimmy, both of them fine-tuned to seismic tremors that signaled a disturbance, turn sharply. Fat Al, Chuckie's-in-Love, and Helicopter Harry were arguing in front of the scar-necked man. Doing their act. Loman realized he hadn't seen the man before tonight. The other three men were telling war stories to him as if competing before a silent, judging audience of the dead.

"LURPS were fairies," Fat Al was saying. "SEALS were queer for their own gear. In Force Recon—"

"Closest he got to Force Recon," Chuckie's-in-Love said, "might'a been feedin' 'em when they came off patrols. Got an earful for their belly-full. Me, I was riverine navy, up the Delta."

"Only deltas he got up belonged to Saigon bar girls, tried to get into the country's dark secrets that way." Fat Al winked at the man. "What's this sailor know? Force Recon, we did Panama Jungle School, Okinawa Northern Training Area, Underwater Demolition, Benning Jump School, Harvard Law. After that the war was easy. Go out with a team, stay out maybe three, four, six weeks along the DMZ, over the line sometimes. Ask Helicopter Harry, he'd extract us."

"Extract me from this shit," Chuckie's-in-Love moaned.

The scar-necked man grinned at all of them, as if he knew their secrets. His eyes gleamed red in the light. The scar, extended up by a shadow, made his face seem split in two, the halves glued back together badly. He said nothing. He fingered his bracelets. Loman moved a little closer, sliding down the bar.

"'This shit'?" Fat Al said in wonder. "You say, 'this shit,' you squid scum?"

"Right, you heard me, I said stop jackin' us off with that Recon shit," Chuckie's-in-Love said.

"I stopped jacking off altogether," Helicopter Harry said mournfully. "Years ago. I just couldn't hack a long-term relationship."

Loman watched them competing, dancing in front of the death's head grin. He moved a little closer. Jimmy went behind the bar. He saw the Germans were eyeballing the vets uneasily. They went back to pinching breasts and thighs, their faces twisted into expressions of disdain as if they were engaged in a contest whose grand prize was self-contempt. He knew he should have been used to them, their beer-hall laughter, but they still seemed out of place to him, jarring to his ears and eyes, even though Bangkok was their place now, the city going backward in its whoring since he'd first come to it on R&R twenty-odd years ago—gone from servicing the soldiers of Vietnam to pandering to the aging troops of the Axis. The Germans looked over at the vets. One of them mouthed the word "Vietnam" softly, as if he'd heard it in Loman's mind. Fat Al swiveled around and glared at him, like a point man for Loman's own dull rise of anger.

"Damn," Helicopter Harry sighed deeply.

The German looked down at the black pilot and said another word to his companions. They laughed unpleasantly.

"'Schwartz' who?" Fat Al said. "What you call Harry?"

The German folded his arms.

Fat Al put a finger under his nose—a Hitler moustache—and gave him the Nazi salute. The German rose unsteadily, ignoring Sahn, one of Loman's best girls, who pulled at his crotch, trying to haul him back down. She looked at Loman. Control your maniacs.

"*Was macht du, Fritzie?*" Fat Al prodded.

The German smiled mirthlessly. His heavy cheeks were streaked with snail trails of sweat. "Vietnam," he said again, putting the word clearly out in the air.

The thin, scar-necked man smiled also. His eyes gleamed.

"Shut the fuck up," Fat Al said.

The German sneered at him. "Vietnam," he said, louder than he had before.

"Watch your foul mouth," Chuckie's-in-Love said.

"Vietnam," the German said once more.

"You've gone too far this time, you Kraut bastard," Fat Al warned. "Take it back."

"Vietnam," the German insisted.

"I'm going to hang my fucking washing," Fat Al said, "on the fucking Siegfried line, man."

"Vietnam," the German said triumphantly.

"D-fucking-day," Fat Al screamed and leapt. The German swept up a bottle from the table and flung it at him. It bounced off his head. Fat Al bulled forward. The German squealed and slapped at him ineffectually. Fat Al grabbed the German's ears, yanked his face down, and brought his own knee up. The other Germans, hung with screaming bar girls, were trying to rise and help. Fat Al twisted the German's head, pushed him to the floor, and fell on him. He clamped his teeth on the German's ear. Loman saw his jaws working, chewing. The man screamed louder than the bar girls. Chuckie's-in-Love got down on his knees and played referee, counting him out. One of the other Germans struggled free and up. "Damn," Helicopter Harry said again, and clubbed him across the nose with a half-empty Singha bottle. The other two Germans put their hands down flat on the tabletop and sat still.

"Loman." Jimmy handed him the bat. Loman shrugged and walked over to Fat Al. The German's cries were getting high-pitched and desperate as he realized no one was going to stop the fight. Loman tapped Al's shoulder once, hard. Al growled and rolled, tearing off a part of the ear, glaring up at Loman like a man interrupted in the middle of a meal. Loman did a neat golf swing into his jaw. Fat Al spit out the bloody morsel, looked at Loman reproachfully, and fell. The German, sobbing, raised himself to his knees and brought both hands above his head. Loman hit him on the forehead, for no good reason at all, feeling a vibration in his hands that sickened him slightly. He saw the scar-necked man smiling at him, his crooked eyes shining. A whiff of sweat and blood and pure jungle rankness filled Loman's nostrils like something leached up from his memory, the hard mud of his heart cracking and letting it leak out.

One of the other Germans, a short, thin man, his face desperate with a decision he'd apparently decided he had to make, came at Loman, a broken bottle in his hand. He was too close, and Loman waited for the slicing pain, thinking, How foolish. A blur flashed in the corner of his eye. He glimpsed the braceleted hand shoot out and strike the German's side. The man's eyes widened; he tried to say something to Loman and fell over, crashing dramatically into the table.

Loman had seen the glint of the knife blade just below the flashing bracelets; it winked open in his mind's eye now, catching up with the action.

"Us," the scar-necked man said, eyes gleaming red, smiling at him like the principle of mischief.

"Shit," Loman said.

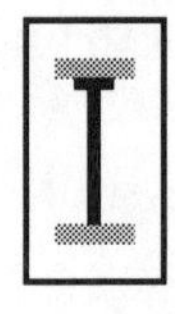he bar looked diminished in the hard light streaming through the open door. Normally Loman liked to let the world in, puncture the night bubble. But this morning he felt threatened.

Captain Krit sighed.

Loman refilled his glass with beer. Krit sipped it with another sigh. The sighing was a new affectation. Loman supposed he was adapting to the mannerisms of his new position. When Krit was a sergeant, he swore and screamed at suspects. Before that he had been a humble, eager young cop in training. None of the stages lasted long. Krit's father was involved in the northern teak trade: he had been a deputy minister just long enough to get a son or daughter, niece or nephew, in every department of the government that could possibly affect his business. Krit was not so much rising through the ranks as being pushed. Loman usually liked him. For a Bangkok cop he was relatively honest, no doubt because he had enough money not to be crooked; he took his job more seriously than his father probably wanted him to. He took it more seriously than Loman wanted him to today.

The policeman put his glass down on the teak counter top, ignoring the coaster Loman had put down. All of the bar's interior woodwork came from Krit's father's company. The coaster said PUT ER THERE, PARTNER and had a representation of buttocks on it. Jimmy, Loman recalled, had ordered two gross of them.

"Don't you find this sort of thing bad for business?" Krit waved languidly at the chalk outline on the floor.

"I won't put it in our brochure."

"You're an amusing man, Loman."

"It's camouflage over a sensitive soul."

"There are people who don't like your soul." Krit tapped the picture on the coaster. "There are people who would like to see it migrate to another existence. People who are not happy with a *farang* owning a business here in the first place."

"I'm only half-owner."

Krit rolled his eyes. "With a Chinese. We have Thai pimps we have to take care of, Loman. Buy Thai."

"I never hear anybody complaining about Sony or Toshiba."

"They trickle down," Krit explained. "The only thing that trickles down from your bar is gonorrhea and AIDS."

"We all contribute what we can."

"You more than most, perhaps. You've met the killer before?"

"No."

"From your description, he sounds like one of your veterans."

"They're not my veterans. They're just customers, like the tourist who was killed."

"Ah, but they're not tourists, are they Loman? They're residents." He giggled. "Residue. Like yourself. And your residence permit is up for renewal, isn't it?"

Loman shrugged, but Krit's threat made him feel sick.

"Look, there was a bar fight. It happens. The man did what he did and disappeared. It's not my responsibility. I never saw him before. Neither did the other guys at his table."

"They know as much as you," he said in disgust.

"They were drunk."

"They were breathing, you may as well say. They were Americans, you may as well say. If I had my way, they would all be on the next plane out." He tilted his head and smiled slightly at Loman, including him in the threat. Loman wondered why he had never seen before how much Krit hated him.

"Leaving would kill them," Loman said, feeling sicker. "They'd be fish out of water."

Krit closed his eyes and smiled as if he found the picture immensely attractive.

You never saw him before?" Loman asked.

Helicopter Harry looked honed down after two days of interrogation, his brown skin faded, taut against his cheekbones. Though Krit, he'd told Loman, hadn't really mistreated him. He'd only kept asking the same question Loman had just asked him.

"The man just showed up," he said, "one of life's little surprises. He seemed to fit."

Harry had said he needed to stretch out after his confinement, so he and Loman walked through the city, an activity that Loman normally avoided if he could. Bangkok was the rest of the world in fifty years: permanent gridlock, the sidewalks thick with people grinning as if caught in a joke they could do nothing about. It was near midday now. Cars, buses, and jitneys moved imperceptibly, like the growth of plants. The exhaust fumes laced with the smells of the meat cooking on sidewalk charcoal braziers; Loman had the sensation that he was smelling his own skin burning. He and Harry pushed through the clots of people as oblivious to the crawl of traffic as they were to the ear-splitting din of unmuffled engines, blaring radios, and shouting vendors. As oblivious as they were to Loman and Harry. They passed a ten-storied glass-walled air-conditioned mall set down like a spaceship or a moral choice in the squalor. Loman saw a traditionally dressed Thai woman staring at a naked mannequin in a shop window. They walked by treasures: spice shops bejeweled with red and yellow chili peppers, cumin, turmeric, and coriander; bronzeware and star sapphires gleaming like the eyes of strange animals from the darkened doorways of small souvenir stores; stalls selling skewers of juicy *sate* and glistening heaps of lychees, golden bananas, mangoes, papaya.

"Why do I have the feeling," Loman said, "that you conjured him up, right there in my bar."

"Our wishes wrapped in flesh," Harry nodded. "That's what Bangkok is for."

In a *soi* off the street, Loman glimpsed the walled compound of a rich family: his eyes fled for relief to the shiny green of the palm fronds showing over the broken glass embedded atop the wall, like the past of the city held preserved in a zoo.

"Bangkok is our woman," Helicopter Harry said. "Everybody says so. The best minds. Like Vietnam was our woman. Like we were the officers' women. Like we were America's women. Like women are our women. No woman ever called me nigger. God is in her heaven, all is right with the world. What an auto-rotating cluster fuck."

"You were an officer," Loman pointed out.

"Warrant officer," Harry said. "It's not the same. We were the regular officers' women."

Harry was the only one of his customers he had actually known during the war. He'd had a reputation as a daring medevac pilot, one of those flyers who seem to become part of their aircraft. But he'd been taken off flight status, from the story Loman had heard, when he changed his call signal to

Charon and started putting coins on his dead passengers' eyes. He flew a corporate Lear for a Swiss quality-control company now.

They stopped in front of a papaya stall. The woman behind the counter *wai*-ed and smiled at them, a nothing-held-back Thai smile, a light breaking under her skin. It was as much a relief to Loman as the sudden green of the palm tree. The song about Taksin was playing on the transistor radio; she hummed the tune as she peeled and chopped two large papayas and put the pieces into plastic bags filled with ice chips. Loman paid her and they kept walking. They picked pieces of papaya from the bags and bit into the sweet pink flesh.

"Papaya is my woman," Harry said, juice running down his chin.

"What could you tell Krit?"

"Not a lot. Tell you the truth, Krit seemed barely interested. Just going through the motions."

"Where did you meet him?"

"Krit?"

"No," Loman said impatiently.

"At his hotel. The Hotel Miami."

Loman told Harry the word the killer had spoken.

Harry stopped. He squinted at Loman, as if he were peering down from his cockpit at dangerous country.

"Jesus," he said, "are you on about that again?"

"About what?" Loman said innocently.

"Us. The fellas. As in 'In Us We Trust.' Come on, Jake, I've heard the stories. The missing are our women," Helicopter Harry said. "Listen, man, the guy could barely squeeze out a sound."

"What do you mean?"

"You see his throat? It must have been shrapnel."

"I heard him."

"Maybe you didn't understand him. Maybe he said 'less.' Less calories. Maybe he said 'ugly.' He was into existential mutterings. I think he was setting himself up as a cult figure. A kind of whorehouse Werner."

"And you told Krit about the Miami?"

"Why not? I don't do cults."

"A *farang* in funny clothes with a funny voice and a scar. He would seem like an easy person to find."

"You care that much about the Kraut he offed?"

"Krit is pressing me. He's threatened to close me down."

Harry shook his head. "Strange tales are told about the Hotel Miami, when the boys gather around their campfires. The lady behind the desk there, name of Kitty, is said to be connected. Pretty Kitty of the front desk. It is said she has many funny friends. Maybe they're too funny for Krit. Maybe he's afraid he'll die laughing."

"Sure. But why is he on me?"

Loman felt a tug at his trousers and looked down. A very young boy with no legs and one withered arm was crab-scrambling around his feet. The boy's stumps were scraped bloody by the filthy concrete of the sidewalk. A claw remnant hand pushed up a cup to Loman and Harry. Loman stuffed some baht into it. Some of the people passing glanced curiously at the foreigners and the torso as if they were witnessing the start of a new fad. Perhaps in his last life the boy had been an evil man, or a lower animal, a vulture who sat perched behind a bar and feasted on the dead. Loman watched the torso drag itself off, scuttling through a world of feet and legs: the jungle where it roamed and made its living.

"Beats me," Harry said.

e have a cash-flow problem," Jimmy said.

Loman poured himself a bourbon.

Jimmy giggled. "They said money is no problem. Those very words."

"I don't do it anymore," Loman said to his glass.

"Man, you promised me you'd talk to them. And that was before we had to mop a dead German from the floor. We got people who are not going to take their bills in 'you-don't-do-it-anymore.' What do you think Krit was saying to you?"

"Krit tells me he could get no information from Harry and the others. But Harry gave him the guy's hotel."

"What's your conclusion?"

"Krit wants money? He never has before. But he is pressuring me."

Jimmy shrugged. "It's working. Look, we've been raided twice, our import liquor is stuck at customs, I can't even get napkins. The girls are getting offers elsewhere. Look, Jake, I have other businesses to take care of."

"I don't do it anymore."

Jimmy nodded at the dancing girl, then waved at the other girls sitting bored at the empty tables.

"Partner, these girls work for you, go to hotels with our customers, lay under them, wiggle, make noises, take baht."

"I'll lay down and wiggle, but I'm too old and ugly to pretend to enjoy it anymore."

Jimmy laughed. "You're a crazy *farang*."

He grinned back at Jimmy, letting himself be whatever Jimmy wanted.

"No one is asking you to enjoy it, man," Jimmy said. "Thing is, they probably just want to say they did it. Wiggling in this case is you take these guys to the jungle, have someone roar and shake some bushes. Mr. and Mrs. Sahib shit themselves, go home happy with real life warm and stinky in their drawers."

Loman finished his drink and poured another.

"I have a man in customs, I can talk to," Jimmy said, "another in the municipality . . . "

"How much do we need?"

A man and a woman walked into the bar. They stepped over the chalk mark and sat at the booth where the German had sat.

Jimmy calculated in his head. "With paying off some bills? Maybe thirty thousand."

"Baht?"

Jimmy laughed politely.

"Just talk to them," he said.

Loman swiveled the stool around and walked over to the booth. Jimmy came behind him.

They were both on the same side of the table, though they sat with perhaps a foot of space between them. The man was Asian, Japanese Loman thought, the woman Western. Watching them in the mirror as he spoke to Jimmy, Loman had not seen any physical contact. They were either business partners or else married for a long time. Or maybe they were just mad at each other. He had no idea what his observation meant except that it made him feel in control.

The man had a comic-book handsomeness. The woman's face, on the other hand, was almost disquietingly real in the way it refused to be classified; a wide, sensuous mouth with its lips held in a tight line, a nose slightly too small for her broad forehead, even her blonde hair, which was drawn into a tight bun, had errant strands sticking out like uncontrollable thoughts. She pushed at it, smiled at Loman, then frowned.

"Sit down and have your drink with us, won't you, Yank? You make me nervous standing there, projecting your little air of menace."

She was Australian.

"He looks like a priest," the Japanese man said. "A well-fed, albeit corrupt, priest."

"Albeit," Jimmy said proudly, rolling his eyes at Loman.

Loman put his drink down on a coaster and sat. Jimmy sat down next to him, smiling. The Japanese man didn't return it. "Sure, Loman's a priest, a *bhikhu*, this his monastery," Jimmy nodded. "Pussy pagoda. Loman, meet Charlene and Usama."

"Charlie and Sam," the woman corrected. She tried a smile like an afterthought.

Journalists, Loman decided. But they were new at it, or rich kids playing at it, representing some obscure lefty journal run on seed money from one of the editor's capitalist parents. Their clothing was too artificially wrinkled, its material too unworn, the Samsonite camera bag on the seat next to Charlene—Charlie—too artfully scratched up on its clean surface. Usama unzipped the bag and took out a video camcorder; he put it on his shoulder and started to focus on Loman.

Loman put his hand on the lens and pushed it down. Usama shuddered, as if his flesh had been violated.

At least they weren't parents, he thought, any more desperate innocents abroad blinking in confusion in the harsh light, looking at him as if he were the last piece of debris from the shipwreck of the war. But the missing were just another illusion, like the ten-minute illusion of love his whores sold. Like he sold his whores. But he did not con his customers, not even the ones who had paid him to take them north, from camp to village to bone merchant until, inevitably, they would arrive at a point, as distinct a destination as an X on a map, when they would come to resent his heresy, hate him for telling them not to waste their money, look at him as if he not only had killed the dream of their sons but their sons themselves.

"We gather you are the man to see," Usama said.

Loman looked at him. "You gather that, do you?"

Charlene raised her hand and shaded her eyes. A large Motok ruby gleamed on her little finger, like the primal source of all the red in the room.

Jimmy shot him a warning glance.

Loman waved at the bar. "I sell drinks. You want a private sex show or a couple's night tour of steamy Bangkok, you get brochures at your hotel. Where are you staying?"

"Hotel Miami," Usama said.

Loman glanced quickly away, to the bar. "I hear it's a good hotel. Well located and convenient to everything: the airport, Thai boxing, massage parlors, cock fights, Thailand-in-Miniature, many pagodas. You want temple tours, fingernail dances, sword fights, and elephants dragging logs, why don't you ask your desk clerk?"

"We understand you have contacts," Usama said, ignoring his speech. "In the north. In the Shans."

"Who the hell are you?"

Charlene said, "Really, what's the difference. You be the tour guide, we'll be the tourists. We want the Taj at midnight, we're paying for it, right?"

"What's the Taj at midnight?"

Maybe they were smugglers looking for a connection, or narcs looking for a bust, or arms dealers, or tourists looking for midnight illusions, he thought. She was right, what was the difference?

"We're making a film," Charlene said.

Loman laughed, he couldn't help it. Why not?

"Look, all we want to do is pick your brain, go up to the border with you, interview some of your contacts who claim to have seen or heard of MIAs. We have our own sources—we have information there were some sightings of MIAs, possibly the ones that call themselves Us, with the Taksin group."

Loman had heard some of the rumors about Americans seen with Taksin. But he felt Taksin himself was probably only a rumor, a wishful thought.

"Taksin is our woman," he said. Charlene looked at him, startled.

Taksin had taken or been given the name of an ancient legendary Thai rebel. There were too many versions of what he was, enough so that Taksin was whatever anyone wanted him to be: an up-and-comer in the opium armies, a student leader—either Thai or Burmese—who had fled to the Golden Triangle and led his students into an alliance with tribespeople, a communist bandit. They were all bar stories as far as Loman was concerned.

"Why?" he asked.

"Why what, mate? MIAs or Taksin or is the sky blue?"

"Why look?" he said.

Charlene looked at him in silence for a moment. "When

was the last time you were back in the States? Your hobby has become a bloody industry. Films, books, organizations of earnest devotees. Lobbyists. Something didn't come back from the war; they're all sure it's out there somewhere, moldering in the jungle, betrayed by politicians, caged in bamboo, pieces of yourself you didn't want to look at too closely."

"Will that line be in your movie?"

Charlene laughed. She brought the ruby up to her mouth and sucked on it.

"It's only stories," Loman said.

"A story is all we want," Usama said.

"We're these story freaks." Charlene patted her unruly hair.

They were bone merchants. Belt-buckle dealers, burnt-uniform salesmen.

"I don't trust stories," he said. "They always have pieces of the storyteller stuck to them."

"That's disgusting," Usama said.

"I don't trust your story," he said to them.

But he wanted their money. And he still wanted to look.

When he managed the E Club at Phu Bai during the war, sometimes the grunts would come in, padding cautiously, their rank smell, their hair so matted with crud it was like fur, their tarnished bracelets, their worn tiger stripes and over-bright, wary eyes intruding like the jungle itself into the fake tropical motif. They would be filthy and loud and twined together around some ancient secret that gleamed way back in their eyes, that gave them a racial alikeness, whether they were black, brown, or white. He would watch them drink and listen to their stories, then he would watch them go back out through the wire as if they were something uncoiling out of himself, disappearing into the waiting jungle like his probe into the kingdom of death, and he would feel an ache as from some vestigial organ to be taken into the fleeting intimacy of that line, that futile linking with each other in the face of the immensity they were entering. Then he would turn to the details of supply and cleaning and decoration, the tallying of figures that kept his mind from wandering like a patrol through the dark, torturous paths of jungle.

Twenty years later what remained to him was a joining image of one long patrol unraveling from his memory, a line of green disappearing into a vastness of green. A yearning.

"Help us," Charlene said.

"I'm not interested," Loman replied.

The driver turned, but Loman couldn't see his face, just the flash of silver aviator glasses and teeth. He reached back over the top of the seat, a steel Rolex dangling on his skinny wrist, spearing more brightness into Loman's eyes. Loman took the brochure. It was mainly in German. There were English and Japanese translations on each opposite page, like the assembly instructions that come with toys or electronic gadgets, but even the English sounded German, couched in the pedantic heartiness of Teutonic fantasy: tours to "study the sexual habits of Asian women." A picture of the German lying on the floor of the bar, his face suffused with wonder, formed in Loman's mind. He looked to see if the Naga Queen was listed on the back of the brochure. It was. The Hotel Miami was not. He refolded the brochure and put it on the seat. The driver's face flashed at him in the mirror. Loman knew most of the cab drivers that came to the bar, but he had never seen this man before.

They were out of the city, driving through the heat-shimmering flatness, past dikes picketed by lines of cone-hatted, sarong-clad women, past the Howard Johnson architecture of the hotels along the highway to the airport. He had not been to the airport since his return to Bangkok from the States the year before. He settled back in his seat and thought about his trip.

It was his first time back in America in fifteen years. It had been a mistake. A congressman named Elliott Mundy had sent Loman a ticket; because of the search expeditions he had been hired to do, his bar's reputation as an information clearinghouse, he was requested to testify before a committee on MIAs chaired by Mundy. Before the hearing, the congressman had taken Loman to lunch and then to the Vietnam memorial as if it were Loman's personal shrine or rather, as if he, a middle-aged ex-REMF were Mundy's ticket to appear before the names of the dead. Mundy, who was Loman's age, apparently felt bad about getting out of the war. At the Wall, he stared at Loman with a hungry silence. He had felt the congressman's need forming into a compulsion in himself to live up to the expectations, to be the mourning vet, have flashbacks, speak to the names, leave offerings, free birds as people did at the Temple of the Emerald Buddha. It annoyed him that the congressman was appropriating emotions Loman had to make up.

The veterans Loman saw at the Wall, in fact—it was crowded, a day before Memorial Day—reminded him of his own Bangkok vets, dressed in overtight or newly bought fatigues, wearing their ribbons and badges and arcana, meeting the expectations of an audience of gawkers, of vicarious players of—in a word—Americans, because it gave them something to be. Us. Their grief was honed to a ritual. Afterward they would buy I WAS THERE T-shirts from the grinning Vietnamese vendors whose trucks lined the nearby streets, who had floated after the vets to fit neatly back into their supporting roles, or they would stare solemnly at the exhibit of the caged POW/MIA, Loman seeing it as if they were looking at themselves. In some ways the whole country had seemed like that to him—

everything from clothing styles that looked like costumes to architecture to music to the president himself—had seemed an acting out on a large scale of some childhood place in the mind that might, or might not, have really existed.

He had walked by the names on the Wall once, not speaking. Then he had walked away. Mundy had come after him, at a respectful distance. He knew all about flashbacks. He was there for Loman.

At the hearing, the congressman had become less solicitous, more in sympathy with the same be-ribboned, MIA-braceleted vets Loman had seen at the Wall. Less sympathetic with Loman. Loman didn't live up to his billing as star witness. The vets were incensed at his insistence that his chases along the border were useless, that there were no survivors, that the basis for their religion, with its shrine, robes, and secret language, was nonexistent. In his heart he wanted the missing to be there; he searched because he wanted to find, not just for the money. His testimony was proof of that, he'd thought—essentially he was putting himself out of the MIA business. The next day he caught the first plane back to Bangkok, where he knew what was expected of him.

"Hotel Miami," the leering driver said.

It looked like the kind of B-grade establishment contracted during the war to be an air-conditioned temporary Valhalla of beer and women for tired souls rotated out of the jungle. It was the kind of hotel where Loman had stayed on his first R&R, a place, he recalled, where he not only had gotten his first dose of Thai clap but also another parasitical infection, a worm that had worked into his skin, into his heart.

In his life this day, the Hotel Miami was a six-storied concrete box painted a sun-scorched green and tiered with cracked balconies that stuck out from it like broken drawers.

He paid the driver and went inside. The lobby was air-conditioned to a bone-chilling cold: there was a ferny odor of mold just under the coolness. A black-and-white television played an image with no sound to an empty semicircle of rattan-framed chairs and settees. Opposite the front door was the door to a barbershop. Inside three girls were clipping hair, talking to their customers, their mouths framing soundless words behind the glass. Next to the shop was the closed door to a snack bar, near it the obligatory jewelry counter exhibiting cut-rate star sapphires. There was no one selling jewelry. The lobby looked so much like a normal Bangkok hotel lobby that it seemed almost like the exhibits Loman had seen in the Smithsonian of everyday American rooms and items: an army barracks latrine, neon signs, a classroom, all somehow translated by the setting to be representative. Loman wiped his forehead. He was sweating in spite of the coolness.

"Can I help you?"

A woman appeared behind the check-in counter. She looked at Loman with a cold reflection of his own surprise. The traditional Thai dress she wore seemed a costume on her. But the clothing didn't work. She was taller and darker than most Thai women, almost Indian-looking: a thin, aquiline nose; lips that echoed the twin heavinesses of her breasts; and large dark eyes.

She repeated her question impatiently.

Loman had prepared a cover story: he was looking for contacts in the north for his teak business. He hoped the direction he mentioned—north, the direction of the Triangle—would stir a reaction. He decided it was hopeless.

"I'm looking for someone named Kitty," he said.

She raised her eyebrows. "I don't sell Kitty here. Take your baht to Patpong. You can buy any girl you want there and call her Kitty."

"I don't want fantasy—just information."

"That," she said, "is a contradiction in terms. What do you want information about?"

"Taksin."

"Taksin," she said, "is where you find him."

The door to the snack bar opened. Men and women filed into the lobby. They were all *farangs*, none of them very old, which would not be unusual in a cheap hotel near the airport. But something about them rolled a shock of coldness through Loman's head. He was a bartender and he had categories, but these people didn't fit anything but each other. They were dressed casually neat: pants suits for the women, sports shirts and slacks for the men, but it wasn't the clothing, nor their silence, that tied them together. It was a wolfish quality. These traveled in packs.

They eyed Loman warily, sniffed in unison, and padded out of the lobby. In the middle of them Loman saw an older face. The man was dressed in a clean white shirt now, but the bracelets were still on his wrists and his eyes gleamed red. He smiled at Loman.

"Wait," Loman called. The woman behind the counter took his wrist and plunged something into his arm. He felt a prick, a burn, and saw her palm the syringe. He turned and watched the file moving through a metal door. He rushed to it. The lobby stretched and came back as he ran. He twisted the knob. It seemed to grow hot and then cold in his hand, then sweat.

That's disgusting, Usama said.

Loman shook his head. He turned to see the woman disappearing through another door. She stopped in its frame and smiled at him. He came after her. A corridor stretched before him, lined with closed doors. She was at the end. Kitty. He started to run. The doors whizzed by, their sequence of numbers holding some code he couldn't break. Their knobs melted when he touched them. He pounded on their cold blank faces but they stayed closed to him. At the end of the hall was the darkness she disappeared into.

He ran after her, his feet weighted, as if he was up to his ankles in muck. Kitty looked over her shoulder and smiled terribly, beckoning. *The corridor was melting at its edges into the street. In front of the closed doors people were sleeping on mats amid the debris, indifferent to the foul gas exploding in their faces from the exhaust pipes of the cars. Crumpled and torn papers skittered and tumbled around them, stained posters and pamphlets, flashes of words and pictures, advertisements for sex tours and bars, a dim photograph of a tiger mounting a woman.*

The woman ran ahead of him, looking back over her shoulder, her eyes gleaming in her dark face. Loman reeled against the walls. A small part of him deep in the cracks twisted in panic.

What was he doing?

The woman was right ahead of him, turning to look, her face mocking.

He was in a seedy Bangkok hotel with a snake turning in his head.

He was walking down a street in Naha, Okinawa, bar door, hotel-room door, bar door, hotel-room door, he needed to organize the shipment of a refrigerator to a province chief with whom he has currency dealings. He stopped and yawned, a huge, out of control yawn that was caught and mirrored exactly by an Okinawan bar girl leaning against a red doorway. Their gazes met and they both laughed as if caught, soldier and bar girl, Loman reading in the mutual yawn, the mutual laughter, a recognition of their total boredom with the lives they had stepped into. The woman's yawn was an opening more intimate than the opening of sex. The woman looked at him and shuddered deeply, seeing a violation of her last inviolate privacy in Loman's eyes, he'd yawn-raped her. She turned and began wobbling away on her spiked heels, wait, he yelled, but when she saw him coming she stripped off the heels and started to run. He ran after bar girl, Kitty, bar girl, Kitty, into an alley, down another street, past the startled faces of whores and soldiers flashing in the lights from the bar signs. Stop, he yelled, and Kitty ran away through the maze of corridors in the Hotel Miami, into a jumbled warren of rickety wooden houses with paper doors and broken tiled roofs, a cobbled street stabbed crookedly into it, a silent, dark jumble of dwellings that existed like props in the darkness behind the neon strip of G.I. bars. She stopped, her eyes locked with his. She tossed her hair angrily and took his arm. Us, she said. Loman suddenly felt a curious passivity, he had chased her and she caught him. She opened a door. She turned to him, her face shadowed and changed. Taksin, she said, is where you find him. Okay, she said. You want, you get. She drew him inside. There was a shrine on a low table: statues, bowls, and vases with joss-stick antennae. Photographs in plastic frames on the walls: sepia prints of old Okinawan men and women in kimonos; a magazine picture of marines watching as Okinawan women, clutching babies to their chests, jump off a cliff into the sea; a room he had fallen into through the crack of a yawn. Satiny, turquoise material had been stapled like wallpaper to the walls. On the walls were Japanese movie stars, a poster of John Lennon. On the dresser were books with Sanskrit letters on their spines. He had walked into someone else's mind. There was a bed. A Japanese tatami that blinked into a queen size. She put her hands on his chest and pushed him to it. She was bigger in the small space, her movements fluid and possessive. She filled the room. She pulled back the cover. What do you wait for? she asked. Loman took off his clothes. With each garment he felt himself disappearing. She watched him indifferently and when he was done patted him impersonally and patted the bed. She looked grim and intent and hungry, the way he imagined a soldier would look to her, at her. Her pat was a gesture of power. He shivered under the sheet. She left the room. He thought she would be naked when she came back. But she wore a white cotton nightgown. Her body glowed through it like a ghost. Her breasts and shrouded black delta swelled with strength. He would not be surprised nor would he resist if she leaned over and bit his neck, he would let himself flow into her mouth, be absorbed in the tissues of her body the way he felt the room absorbing him. He started to move forward, but she said no, sharply, and grasped the sides of his head, pushing, directing, her nails biting sharply into his head. Something coagulated in his head, loosened and bled out. She closed her eyes, her face completely closed into itself, as he did what she wanted. Something shifted inside himself, as if he had been entered and changed. She pulled at the back of his skull. Good, she said coldly. More, she said. There, she said. Taksin, she said. Her tastes ran into him, stained his heart. He floated up. He hovered above the entwined figures like a waiting soul watching its own conception.

The old air conditioner in the window rattled busily and aspirated its moldy, visible breath of cold air. Sahn arched her body in the cold stream. She gave a grunt of satisfaction and rolled over. Her back was streaked with sweat. She worried a pimple on one buttock. Loman watched the sweat cool and evaporate on her skin. He was grateful for her solidity. He rested the cold bottle of Singha on his chest, gripping it with one hand, cupping his beer gut with the other as if making a visible or symbolic connection. Sahn turned her head, looked at his body, and frowned.

"Loman, you getting too fat." She wiggled her slim, cool fanny at him, as if to show off the contrast. He felt a tug of response that surprised him. Human beings. The paunchy white man, the brown native girl, the stripes of light coming through the bamboo curtain, the shoddy apartment with its overhead fan and lizard scampering up the wall: he felt stuck in a scene from someone's hackneyed daydream.

He walked over to the window and looked out, leaning over the air conditioner, to Sahn's whimpered protest. His apartment was in the rear of the building. People lived in the garbage-strewn, weedy lot behind it like stage workers behind the scenes. The thought caused something to shift in his head and for a second he was still running down the endless corridors of the Hotel Miami. He looked down at the lot behind his building, anchoring himself in its reassuring squalor. A canal filled with scummy green water cut a border through the tangle of weeds and trash, but it only divided one warren of corrugated-tin lean-tos and packing-crate dwellings from another. From above, he could see into the open end of a lean-to, as if it were an exhibit in a museum of slums. A family was squatting and eating from bowls in their laps, their hands moving rapidly to their mouths. They looked happy and domestic. No one looked up at him looking down.

"Too fat," a voice said, Sahn of course, but for an instant, dazed with heat and beer, it was as if a voice from the shacks below had leaked into the sealed capsule of his existence. Sahn reached up lazily and kneaded his backside. "Too fat," she muttered again. "Too heavy." Her hand fluttered around to his belly, grabbing his flesh as if the fatness was something she wanted to take.

There was a knock on the door. Loman pulled on a pair of shorts. Sahn sighed, but otherwise didn't stir. The knocking grew louder. "Hold on," Loman called.

He opened to Jimmy's smile. It twisted into an automatic male leer, a pimp's smile of approval, when he saw Sahn. As long as this went on, there would be business.

"Unsatiated," Loman said, quoting the Buddha, "all beings are slaves of lust."

Jimmy sat down at the card table that served as Loman's dining-room furniture. "Tell me how it went. Talk to me as if I was your partner."

Loman went to the compact refrigerator in the kitchen alcove. "Do you want a beer?"

"No, man."

He took one for himself. He didn't know what to tell Jimmy: he wasn't sure himself how much of it was real after he'd been drugged, for that matter there wasn't a clear line or sequence in his head about any of the events in the Hotel Miami. The touch of Kitty's flesh lingered in his mind like a real memory, but what was that?

Jimmy pulled a deck of cards out of his pocket like a magician, shuffled, began laying a solitaire build.

Loman drank the beer. His head was still hollow and aching. When he had come back to himself yesterday, the horn-tipped roofs and cob-shaped *prangs* of the temple of the Emerald Buddha had shimmered into existence in front of his eyes. His shoes had been taken off. Silence was gathered around him like a monk pulling his robes to himself. Near him, Japanese tourists muttered excitedly to each other, pointing out praying Thais, as if they were a group from Terre Haute who found Buddhism exotic. In front of Loman, a slight girl in a sarong sitting with her legs folded under her, bent her head and *wai*-ed three times, bringing her steepled hands from mat to forehead. An old woman passed, selling incense sticks. Loman bought one and lit it and placed it in the sand in front of the Buddha. He sat cross-legged on the matting and closed his eyes and tried to meditate. He prayed that when he opened them, he would still be in the bot, that his mind had not been shifted permanently out of time. He breathed slowly, concentrating on his breath.

Out-breath one.

In-breath two.

Out-breath three.

In-breath four.

Out-breath five.

Gain.

Loss.

Fame.

Defame.

Praise.

Blame.

Pleasure.

Pain.

When he had opened his eyes, the Japanese were looking at him with approval. He got up, got a taxi to the bar, and took Sahn immediately to his apartment.

"Was this Kitty there?" Jimmy asked.

"Maybe. There was a woman at the desk, I think it was her. But I couldn't get anything out of her."

Jimmy shrugged. He flipped more cards, staring at them as if his and Loman's future were in their pattern. The cards still face down showed what was sometimes called the act of love, in all its physical varieties and contortions, rows of bodies carrying out their illusion of unlimited choices. Loman picked up one of the cards: its back depicted a girl engaged in an almost yogic act of self-caress. He flipped it over. The ace of spades.

"Death?" Jimmy asked, as if he were giving Loman a choice.

Loman looked over at Sahn. She was sleeping, snoring lightly.

"There's someone else who wants to see you," Jimmy said.

The permanent gridlock of cyclos, motorscooters, taxis, jitneys, and cars filled the street with its arrested riot. On the sidewalks people milled, screamed, pushed, as if acting out the frustration of the vehicles. The heat was packed like wet, living flesh between the buildings. It pressed to Loman's own skin until he wanted to dissolve into it, his inside rind touching the thing itself. It multiplied in red-hot exhaust pipes and the hot red glow of the charcoal in the street braziers and the stinging smell of hot chili peppers simmering in bubbling oil and sizzling skewers of meat. Rows of flattened and dried octopi, open like kites, flapped at him in dry rustles.

Loman walked dazed. He stopped in the King Bar, a competitor, and let the vets who lived in the shadows, stuck in a Twilight Zone curse of endless R&R, buy him drinks and tell him their stories that endlessly evoked the dead and killed them again with lies until the dead, pissed off, came into the bar and sat on stools and stared, their young dead faces transparent, the ruby light of the bar glowing hotly behind their pale flesh. They fondled scared bar girls and were fondled in turn, their rank, dead smell growing fouler as they got excited.

Loman got a hat, got out of there, the vets calling after him as if he had betrayed them. *Kon Ahn Harm Kon Die*, the Shans called him, after he'd made three or four trips to the Triangle chasing the missing. The One Who Carries the Dead. But when he started drinking with them, it was time to leave.

Whatever had happened to him in the Hotel Miami was still sliding around in his mind like a piece of loose cargo, jarring him from time. On the street, beggars, their mutilations a memory-catalog of the wounded and dead he had borne on stretchers when, driven by REMF guilt, he had volunteered to help unload the helicopters, clutched at him, clutched at his legs again. An old whore, her face as painted as the face of a corpse, grabbed at his crotch, her smile mocking, as if she were the final form achieved by the fresh-faced girl he had bought out of a bar for six days when he had first come here in '66 and had not yet realized he was stepping into his occupational specialty. That year the teenaged kids were coming out of the jungle, necking in the booths of the bars as if they were in the back seats of Chevvies, walking down the streets of Patpong holding hands with girls as young or younger than themselves, kids who like themselves had been given numbers instead of names, who had been called down from the hill country, from farms and from city slums, to serve the war. As they now served him. A good and fair pimp.

He turned right and felt a childish triumph at seeing the building where it was meant to be; he was to meet Jimmy's new potential client here. It was a four-storied concrete block, a part of the Ministry of the Interior where people went to get their visas extended. He wondered if the person were connected to Krit, the meeting here a symbolic warning.

He sat at the edge of a bench. A slight breeze made the tin awning flap and groan. The old woman next to him smiled with a betel-nut-red mouth that he suddenly saw as the dim ancestral memory toward which the whore who had grabbed him before painted herself. Next to her a group of young, skinny men were playing cards and spitting in the dust, Malaysians or Singaporeans. There were no Vietnamese. They were up the coast, kept behind barbed wire in the camps. Pieces of himself he didn't want to look at, moldering. Numbers were called and people got up and went into the door. Someone would call his number and he'd go inside and find himself in front of a tribunal presided over by a lady judge, an angel of whores, a Sonia of the Orient who never forgot, never forgave.

"Excuse me, are you American?"

The speaker was a young black woman. She didn't mean to alarm him, she explained; she was one. An American, she meant. Loman made a space for her.

From Virginia, she said. She had married a Thai boy she'd met at college. It had been very sudden and surprised both of them. She was here to get her six-month visa renewed. It was difficult to fit into his family, but she was trying; she came from a large family herself, but of course there was some cultural shock. His mother wanted to supervise every moment of her life. There was a kind of mine field she had to thread through daily, not sure if she would violate a custom, if her teasing would fall into the parameters of their teasing or go over a line she didn't know about and be offensive. There was also no privacy. Her husband's brothers and sisters peeked at her in the toilet. But she was too much of an outsider not to be aware of everything, so she just couldn't relax in it. Did he know what she meant? It was like she had gone back to the States after her first six months, to this little town in Virginia she was from? Nothing had changed. But what she couldn't help noticing were all the telephone and power wires criss-crossing in the air. This was a maze so thick that if you flew, say, fifteen feet in the air, you'd be decapitated. They had always been there. But all her life she had never noticed the wires. But coming back, there they were. How could you not notice something like that? Yet after a few weeks home, they were gone again. Did he know what she meant? She was feeling out of it just now. But she knew she would be all right. It would just take time before she would no longer notice the difference.

A soldier came out of the building and called a list of numbers. The young woman got up and went inside. Apparently she wasn't Loman's contact. He sat and looked at the door until she came out again, smiling, holding her passport. She *wai*-ed to the soldier at the door, waved gaily at Loman, and disappeared down the street, into Asia. Straining his eyes, searching after her, Loman felt a bone-deep ache of envy that she had no crimes made visible by her skin or her sex, that for her the wires could disappear.

To call the middle-aged man who sat next to him now a white man would be literal: the man's paleness was almost sickly, sluglike in the green-tinted light under the awning; it was the kind of whiteness that made his close-cropped red hair look like a rash on his scalp. His forearms looked surprisingly thick and strong, with irregular red patches on them, as if he'd had tattoos removed. The man held out his hand. Loman shook it. It was either that or leave it hanging there. The flesh was cold and dry, vaguely reptilian. The checkered trousers both reassured and bothered Loman. Every CID man or spook above a certain age that Loman had ever known had seen checkered pants as the ultimate in mufti.

"Who was the black girl?" the man asked.

"Who are you?"

The man laughed. "Come with me please, Mr. Loman."

His car was a Pinto. In Saigon the GIs had called them Company cars. It was parked illegally behind the building. Loman got in and sat down.

There was a surprisingly solid thunk for a small car when the man got in and closed his door. He started the motor and turned the air conditioner on full blast. He left the car in neutral. He said nothing, just sat and let the treated air fill the interior until the windows fogged. When it was so cold that Bangkok had become a misty dream outside the glass, the man turned to him.

"Arthur Weyland," he said.

"Who are you with—CIA, DEA?"

"Nary an acronym, Mr. Loman. I've retired from all initials. I work on a private, consulting basis for Congressman Mundy. I believe you've met the good congressman."

And now his factotum, in his checkered pants, in his bulletproofed sealed Pinto, had descended into the atmosphere of Loman's world and scooped him up.

"What does Mundy want?"

"Your assistance. Your expertise," Weyland said flatly, without belief.

"I'm just a barkeep."

"Is that a fact?" Weyland asked with interest. His eyes crinkled with amusement. "Let me give you the facts. Jacob Loman," he said. "U.S. Army, 1962–1973. Highest rank, staff sergeant. Three tours, Vietnam, one with an advisory group in 1964, but all tours essentially as a noncombatant. In the rear with the gear. Court-martialed April 15, 1972. Charges: blackmarketeering, currency violations, conduct unbecoming a soldier. To wit: while manager of the Enlisted Man's Club, Phu Bai, Republic of Vietnam, Staff Sergeant Loman did engage in trade with U.S. Government supplies to illegal local elements for monetary profit. To wit, that Staff Sergeant Loman did engage in the illegal changing of American currency for Military Payment Certificates and Vietnamese currency. To wit, that Staff Sergeant Loman owned and operated illegal off-limits establishments for the purposes of gambling and prostitution. Sentence: ten years hard labor, forfeiture of all pay and allowances, and a dishonorable discharge. Prison time and DD suspended in exchange for a general discharge because of the defendant's cooperation with an on-going investigation."

"Yeah, but I never killed anyone."

Weyland laughed. He found Loman the most amusing man in Bangkok. "And you're proud of that."

"Actually," Loman said, "I am. What can I do for you?"

"The facts," Weyland said again, as if he were considering the phrase. "But you and I know there are no facts, don't we? Only perceptions. You're here, as usual, because you're all we have."

"The last time someone said that to me, I was drafted." Loman decided to continue to be amusing. He wondered if Weyland and Mundy had any connection to or knew about Charlene and Usama. Jimmy hadn't known who Weyland was, only that he was talking about a lot of money. It seemed diplomatic not to mention Charlene and Usama.

"This time also."

Loman waited. He was getting tired of Weyland's cryptic statements.

"Reformed sinners are in vogue," Weyland explained. "Weepers. Shitters in their own mess gear. You created a stir in Washington. Negative spin, in the idiom. Your sleaziness made you real. The let's-kiss-and-make-up crowd seized on your testimony as if it were the Word. If there are no MIAs, relationships with the old enemy can be normalized. You see, you're part of the wrong pattern in too many people's heads, barkeep. You're the skeptic who needs to be publicly converted. As publicly as possible."

Loman reached for the doorhandle. Weyland's hand seized his wrist with surprising quickness and strength.

"Let go of me or I'll break your fingers," Loman said. His own anger surprised him. The surprise was that what Weyland had said could still get to him. Weyland smiled as if reading Loman's mind.

"You'll stay," he said. "And you'll do what I want. You'll do that, barkeep, because I have my own connections and because you have a bar you'd like to keep."

"Krit works for you," Loman said.

"Krit who?"

"What do you want?"

"Mundy is here. You might have guessed that. He's on a fact-finding mission about the MIAs, but it's unofficial. The mission will remain unofficial until he is sure there are facts to find. You'll help him find the facts."

"There are no facts," Loman said. "Only perceptions."

Weyland smiled and nodded, as if at a bright student.

Loman had not been joking when he told Weyland he was proud of never having killed anyone in the war. When he first went to Vietnam, in the early sixties, he was a supply clerk assigned to the Military Assistance Command. He was a reluctant supply clerk. He dreamed of slogging with the infantry, his cartridge belt dangling with heavy male instruments of death; of jumping with the airborne, of running swift, silent, and deadly with the Rangers. But the slot had opened and he let himself slide into it. In those advisory days only officers and senior NCOs and helicopter crews were getting into combat anyway, and Loman figured once he was there he could volunteer for patrols, even go AWOL to the fighting; he'd heard stories of people doing that.

That year the Viet Cong had begun their general uprising in the countryside, but they were still a poorly armed force, their standard weapons sawed-off .22s, slingshots, crossbows, and C-ration cans converted to booby traps. The American strategy was to train and equip the Army of the Republic of Vietnam to an American model, a mirror image, only smaller. Like a penis, only smaller, his C.O. Colonel Hawkins explained at his initial briefing, then sighed when Loman didn't get the reference. The American GIs were there essentially to be mirrors, Hawkins told him: each American was issued an individual Vietnamese to form into his image. Hawkins had a parallel colonel named Quang. Loman was given a corporal named Trung, a draftee some fifteen years older than himself, who would smile at him constantly. It was a broad smile, full of gold teeth, but there was a secret mirth behind it that irked Loman. He felt he was still missing the joke.

But he did well. He had already learned the army trick that if you acted sure enough about anything, people would assume you knew what you were talking about. He soon learned the other trick of growing into your own fake. He became very good at supply. His particular job had to do with weapons inventory and distribution. Thousands of M-14s, M-79 grenade launchers, M-60 machine guns, and other weapons were pouring into the country as if someone had overturned a cornucopia of death. Loman came to see himself as the funnel, a tight little ring everything had to flow through. It was an attitude he tried to instill in Trung. We're the rectum, Loman told him: bowel analogies seemed to go over well in Asia. Trung smiled at him. "As you wish," he said.

Loman showed his Vietnamese reflection all his intricately devised inventory programs and fall-back systems. Although he still yearned for action, he was content with competence and responsibility: he was twenty years old and he was running a multimillion-dollar system. He learned to do bar graphs, flow charts, computer tracking, how to conduct really professional briefings. He was promoted to sergeant, staff sergeant, tapped for Officer Candidate School. Trung smiled with great sympathy at his energy. Then one day in a fluent, colloquial English that he had always kept hidden, Trung told his American counterpart not to sweat it so much. Most of the weapons he was keeping such careful track of were simply being sold to the highest bidder by Quang, and in most cases, the highest bidder was the VC. Loman's systems were simply being used as an elaborate cover-up. Anyway, Trung said, the colonel was only doing what his superiors and subordinates were doing. Even when weapons somehow got down to ARVN soldiers in the field, the men were either selling them directly to the VC or abandoning them to avoid trouble.

Loman did what anyone would do after being told that the job he did well and enjoyed and which was giving him esteem and promotion was at bottom false and rotten. He refused to believe it. When he looked up Trung's file and found the Viet had in fact taught economics at Hue University, he was certain Trung was an enemy agent. But still, Trung's words worked at him. There had been certain discrepancies, areas for which he could not account. He decided to go to Hawkins with his suspicions. But that night, the base was hit by a VC battalion.

The attack was broken by American aircraft. In the morning, Loman volunteered himself and Trung to go out with the troops policing the battlefield. Helping to stack the enemy bodies and equipment, Loman experienced déjà vu. He had handled these weapons before. Their serial numbers looked up at him like old friends. He looked at the bodies he was piling on one side and the weapons he was piling on the other and saw how they were interchangeable. Trung, who was helping him, smiled at the look on Loman's face and this time Loman felt the smile grow on his own. He finally got the joke. You couldn't have a war until you armed the other side. There was nothing, Loman decided, dumber than a whore who didn't know he was a whore. When he was finished laughing, he went into business with Trung. Later, on his second and third tours, when he had managed to get into the lucrative Enlisted, NCO, and Officers' Club business, Trung stayed his supplier.

It seemed he had been wrong about the Vietnamese. Trung wasn't a VC. He was an entrepreneur. He had just been waiting for Loman to see the light.

Elliott Mundy was waiting in the lobby of the Dusit Thani. He was tall and slim and dressed in what Loman took to be congressional mufti: a Filipino *barong tagalog* shirt and khaki pants. He looked cool and comfortable. There was no reason Loman could think of why he wouldn't. Mundy had been one of the youngest representatives ever elected to the House. He was the same age as Loman, but he was young and promising, while Loman was middle-age and decrepit. The congressman was elected from a Tidewater district that had his family name stamped on it like an ownership label. He had the connections to keep up the fine old Tidewater tradition of never allowing the naval base that was the life of the area's economy to be closed or moved. His getting out of military service during the war sometimes jarred with his hawkish stance on defense spending. But the people in his district had apparently decided they could live with it. Besides, he had a good deal of what Loman had heard described in news programs when he was in Washington as media visibility.

Mundy made brilliant eye contact with Loman and held it like a belief all the way across the lobby. His hair was a little longer than Loman remembered, swept in a brown wing over Mundy's forehead. The congressman shook Loman's hand, squeezing a little to let Loman feel his firm grip.

"It's good to see you again, Jake."

"Why's that?"

Mundy laughed appreciatively. "Why don't we get a drink?"

They walked to the terrace overlooking the Chao Phraya. An awning-shaded boat full of tourists, naked brown kids playing in its wake like sleek dolphins, passed too close to the terrace wall. Cameras clicked from it like a chorus of locusts. Mundy smiled in automatic response. A waitress Loman knew, an Akha girl who was a graduate of the Derby King, wai-ed and smiled at him. "Jake, how you?" she said, wiggling happily, and Loman saw Mundy glance at Weyland as if his reception by a friendly ex–bar girl showed how connected he was. Loman saw Weyland's face tighten with contempt as if it registered what Loman had thought. The look suddenly made him feel almost sorry for Mundy, protective. It also made him reassess their relationship. Ang, the waitress, led them to a table. At the next table some people Loman knew were from the American embassy's information office looked at Mundy, played his features against some inner file, then whispered excitedly to themselves.

Weyland had seen their glance also. He went over to the table, put his hands possessively on its edge, and whispered to the group. They nodded eagerly, got up, and moved to another table, smiling at Mundy as they left. He smiled back graciously, but his smile was fixed.

"I hope, Art . . ." he started. Weyland raised his hand.

"No need, sir. As far as they're concerned, you're strictly a tourist. Everything will be taken care of."

Mundy stared at him.

"If you say it, I'm sure it will be so." He kept looking at Weyland. "Thank you, Art," he said. "Now you wouldn't mind leaving us for a while, would you?"

Weyland said, "Don't you think this is something I should be here for?"

"I'll fill you in completely. I promise you."

Weyland gave him a murderous glance, but turned and left.

Mundy was still smiling. He made it into a smile of complicity at Loman.

"Would you care for something to eat?"

"Just a drink."

Mundy raised his hand; Ang appeared. Power magic. "I'll have a Beefeater with Schweppes," Mundy said. "Light on the Beefeater."

Ang looked at Loman. "Singha," he said.

They waited in silence until she brought back the order. Mundy leaned forward, as if drawing Loman into his confidence.

"Art Weyland has made a career on the Hill of being everybody's image of the secret agent. I hope he hasn't overdramatized."

Loman raised his glass. "Congressman, you're buying. Why don't you tell me what you want, and I'll let you know if it's for sale."

Mundy's smile was growing a little tired. Loman didn't blame it.

"You don't like me," Mundy nodded, as if that were fair enough. "And I can't say that I blame you. Many of the vets I've met associate me at first with the kid I was, the kid who used his father's influence to get out of the war. Mr. Loman, they're right to look at me that way. I made the wrong decision when I was in my twenties and I've come to regret it. And not only, believe it or not, because I've come to feel that I owed it to my country to go to Vietnam and take my chances, but even more because I feel I missed the quintessential defining experience of our generation."

Loman shrugged. "You've heard all the stories," he said. "Now you want one of your very own."

Mundy's eyes grew opaque. "Who the fuck do you think you are?"

The question made Loman think of the Hotel Miami. He shuddered.

"I want to do something, Loman, to help heal a wound,"

Mundy said, answering his own question. "I owe that." The look of need in his eyes made Loman turn away; he felt like he had opened the wrong door in a whorehouse.

"What exactly do you want from me?"

"I'm sure Weyland told you some of it."

"Let me hear it from you."

Mundy steepled his hands, his eyes fixed to Loman's. "Stories," he said. "In Washington last year, you told of stories you'd heard about American MIAs who were free—they had escaped or had been let go—but who were afraid to come home and were working with opium armies in the Triangle: the group sometimes called Us. You dismissed those stories—as you did all the stories—as wishful thinking. But my own information tends to reinforce their reality. Confirmed sightings, eyewitness accounts of Westerners who meet the age requirements working with Aung Khin's band."

The lean, scarred man formed in Loman's mind, his eyes glowing, an image superimposed over Mundy's earnest gaze as if conjured by it. But Mundy had said nothing about Taksin, and Aung Khin was as real as a virus. Loman dealt Charlene and Usama, the Hotel Miami to the back of his mind, cards he might use later.

"Where is your information from?"

"Oh, some might discount Art Weyland as a comic anachronism. But he has vast experience, in Vietnam and in northern Laos during the war, here in Thailand: he still has many contacts among the hill tribes, particularly the Hmongs."

Loman said, "And you're determined to believe him. Look, you have Weyland and the Hmongs; what do you need me for?"

"Your experience is more recent. Besides, you're the skeptic that has to be convinced."

"Weyland mentioned that. In just about those words."

Mundy took a long drink. He put the glass down and stared at Loman. "Well that makes it clear then, doesn't it?"

"I still don't know what you want me to do."

"Weyland will fill you in on the details. I just need to hear you agree on general principles."

"Sure," Loman said.

"I also understand your establishment is a kind of center for the veterans' community here in Bangkok. I always like to go to the center of things. I'd like to meet some of your friends. Perhaps they can be helpful."

Loman thought about Fat Al, Helicopter Harry, and Chuckie's-in-Love sitting around like permanent adolescents telling war and pussy stories as a center of the veterans' community. He sighed. "I've been getting pressured by the government, about the bar. I mentioned it to Weyland. He thought you could help. That's besides any payment we're talking about."

Mundy looked over the railing at the Chao Phraya and squinted. "Those people over there, from the embassy? They threw a party for me, my first night in Bangkok. They're eager as hell to provide assistance. I don't want a damn thing to do with them, Loman. I'll do what I can for you; you have my word. But I don't want anything funneled through the Thais, or through the embassy. I don't want dogs, or ponies, or shows. Okay? Just between us guys, right? I need people around me I can trust. Do you see?"

Mr. Smith goes undercover. Mundy would get together with the guys at the center of the veterans' community, they'd bond, maybe all go together, a band of brothers, northward to the jungles of his mind. "As you wish," he said to Mundy. The words were Trung's words to him, when Trung had agreed that he was an asshole, during Loman's quintessential defining experience.

How can I explain the atmosphere to you, Loman?" Weyland said. "You have to be there. We're going through an amazing period. We're finding ourselves, as they say. What we're about. What we're about turns out to be entertainment. It's what we're good at. Not cars, but car chases. Not wars, but war movies. Our informational, postindustrial global role is apparently to provide amusement and the mythical underpinnings, if you follow my drift. Never mind, it pays well and it doesn't take heavy machinery. That's where you come in. Entertainment."

The young couple on the stage finished their fourth copulation and stepped out of their intricate, Indian-temple entwinement with a wet, sucking noise. They bowed politely to the audience. Loman saw Fat Al clap Mundy on the back and whisper in his ear. The two of them laughed loudly. Helicopter Harry winked balefully at Loman. The three girls in their laps were talking to each other, Loman could just overhear, about a movie they had seen the night before, their hands absently fondling as if they were a ladies' knitting bee at its gossip. Mundy looked dazed and happy.

"He's an idiot," Weyland said. "But he's my idiot."

"The only idiot you have," Loman nodded. "What do you want me to do?"

Weyland waved at Mundy, who beamed and waved back. "What do you know about Aung Khin?" he asked, his eyes fixed to Mundy as if afraid a lack of attention would cause the congressman to disappear.

"In all the rumors I've picked up, I never heard any mention of Aung Khin and MIAs."

"Something like that," Weyland suggested, "can be suspicious in itself."

"All of the rumors have to do with Taksin." Loman extended the name like a piece of meat shoved before a cage.

Weyland pointed the bottom of his beer bottle at Loman. "What the hell is a Taksin?"

The customer is always the customer. For whatever reason, Weyland apparently had his heart set on Aung Khin. There were no facts, only perceptions. Weyland was in the entertainment business. Still, Loman didn't see why he couldn't continue with Charlene and Usama, double the profit. They were entertainers also. Weyland raised the bottle to his lips and took a swig. "Aung Khin," he said dreamily.

For some reason, Trung's gold teeth came into Loman's mind. The longer the Americans were there, the more gold teeth. He figured that Trung's mouth was one of the few good things that came out of the war.

"Aung Khin," Weyland said, "was born in Lashio, his father Chinese, his mother supposedly a Shan *Sawbaw*'s daughter. She gave him a Burmese name even though—or maybe even because—his father was killed fighting the Burmese. The story is the mother was a great beauty who remarried a Kuomintang general who'd brought his surviving troops into the Triangle after he lost to the communists. Aung Khin was a teenager at the time. He learned the opium trade with the KMT Third Army, and he was regarded as the prime heir to its leadership."

"I've heard all this," Loman said. "I'm your hired expert."

He knew this about Aung Khin. In October of 1949, Chiang Kai-shek's Kuomintang army was defeated by Mao, and retreating nationalist units crossed the border of Yunnan province into Burma, finding refuge in the Mong Hsat mountains. The Chinese KMT soldiers were remnants, survivors, MIAs who took women from the local ethnic groups—Lahu, Yao, and Shan—to wife and got into the drug trade. During the fifties they took over territory throughout northeast Burma. Both Taiwan and the United States saw the KMT remnants as a blocking force against further Chinese communist expansion into Southeast Asia, and even as a possible invasion army to retake the mainland. For a time the KMT was supplied by both Taipei and Washington. KMT troops tried twice to penetrate Yunnan, but each time they were bloodied and sent back, two Asian Bay of Pigs too distant and too yellow for the American public to get excited about. Finally, they simply settled into their stronghold in Shan State, allying with the Karen, Mon, and Shan rebellions against the Burmese government. In 1953 the Burmese army, the Tatmadaw, pushed the KMT back across the Salween River, back into the jungles and mountains of the Golden Triangle. Faced with the annihilation of its surrogate army, Taiwan repatriated six thousand troops and their families. But Aung Khin, his stepfather, and at least another six thousand soldiers stayed hidden in the hills.

His stepfather and mother both died in the Burmese 1961 offensive, which shoved the KMT farther back into the Thailand and Laos corners of the Triangle. Aung Khin joined the 93rd Division of the Third Army, operating in the wild country west of Chiang Mai. Not a happy subordinate, he clandestinely recruited among the Shans and his stepfather's soldiers, until he finally broke away with his own force. Khin's and the other KMT armies, seasoned, well trained and armed, had gained control of most of the Golden Triangle's opium traffic by the early seventies. Khin's group emerged as the biggest and strongest: an opium army that stayed in business as much through political savvy as by force of arms: he maintained the Shan rebellion against Rangoon, kept Thai politicians and generals in his pocket; there were rumors of deals with Langely. Loman figured this as Weyland's connection: figured Weyland was old, bad company during the CIA's salad days in Indochina.

"What do you want me to do, with Aung Khin?" he asked.

"Go to Burma and see him."

"Whatever for?" Loman had in the past, before 1988, made frequent trips to Burma. He found the country's lack of frantic modernization restful after Bangkok; he even had had a certain sympathy with the Burmese government's attempt to isolate the country from the rest of the world. But he hadn't wanted to go back since the democracy demonstrators were shot down on the streets of Rangoon by the army; he'd watched the scenes on the news, and Burma had joined a number of other places he preferred not to even think about anymore.

"You go to Burma," Weyland repeated. "You check in at the Inya Lake Hotel. You wait. Aung Khin will send someone to meet you, take you north to his camp."

Loman thought of his shoving the meat into the cage analogy. "I thought we go together. And why can't it be from Thailand?"

"I thought we told you, Loman; this is unofficial. Official is going through Thai channels so we have to fill every Thai official's rice bowl and we'll still end up with press coverage before we want it. We—and I have to tell you, Aung Khin himself insisted on it this way—want you to liaise with the big guy before we do. 'Liaise' is Mundy's word." Weyland nodded as if that summed Mundy up.

"You want me to stick my head into the cage, see if anything bites it off."

Weyland smiled. "Aung Khin checks you out, he gives you the coordinates, you call us collect. But as far as anyone else is concerned, this is something you've done on your own. The prodigal son finds the truth about MIAs on his own and repentently brings it to Mundy, who happens to be in Bangkok on vacation."

Entertainment, Loman thought.

"I want to take some people with me," he said. He told Weyland about Charlene and Usama, without mentioning their interest in Taksin. Mentioning Taksin seemed to bother Weyland.

Weyland squinted at the stage. Two girls were engaged in a strip swordfight.

"You are out of your mind," Weyland said.

"They give me a good excuse for going, with their film. Cover. And coverage. The whole thing is documented. There can be no skeptics."

Weyland drummed his fingers on the table, thinking about it. "And you collect two fees."

"Do you want a cut?"

Weyland laughed. "How you go and with whom is up to you, Loman."

"Good. How do I let you know when it's okay?"

"I'll give you a radio and a frequency; you can play secret agent."

"Why do I have to carry equipment? Khin must have something I can use."

Weyland sighed. "Hell, the man won't even talk to me on the phone, Loman. Story is, he got ambushed once by the Burmese; they found him by triangulating his radio communications. Then he once got arrested by the Thais; they bugged his phone system. Since then he relies on more traditional methods of communication. Messengers. Drum beats, for all I know. Look, he insisted on doing it this way, so we humor him, Loman. You go. We wait for you somewhere near Chiang Mai, on the Thai side. You scope things out. You get scoped out. You arrange time, date, coordinates. You signal his location to us. And then the good congressman descends from the heavens with gifts and blessings."

Loman regarded him. "How does he descend?"

"Come on, Loman, the guys leapt at the chance, all of them. It's a wet dream for them."

"Leave them out of it. Especially leave Harry out of it."

"He's a pilot and a good one and we'll need to helicopter to you, wrap this up fast," Weyland said. "Look, I told you we need to keep this private, among friends. Besides, you really want to take this away from him, barkeep? Mundy's the only chance Harry has too."

They were both looking at Mundy. He was laughing with Fat Al, bouncing the girl on his lap, his hands grasping, pulling, pinching. Fact finding.

"R&R," Weyland said.

Mundy settled back in his seat, adjusting the girl sitting on him as he would trousers binding his crotch. Fat Al, Helicopter Harry, and Chuckie's-in-Love looked at him, smiling strangely. The girl in his lap and the girls in theirs looked at him. He had just given his speech on how much he regretted not having had the chance to go. That he was a victim of the fashions of his youth and class. Nobody said anything. He closed his eyes and swayed, opened them and grinned ruefully. He could see that they were taking the speech as a speech and waiting for it to be over and he felt at a loss, suddenly afraid he was unable to speak the language of men.

He noticed, as if he were a spectator behind his own eyes, that the room seemed to be spinning slowly. Maybe he was drunker than he thought.

"I admit it," he said. "I sandbagged it."

"Tell you what, senator," Fat Al said, leaning forward, peering at him in the dim red light. Mundy waited, but when Fat Al spoke it was in Thai to his girl, a kid so skinny she looked like an appendage unfolding out of his huge belly, black-and-blue track marks on her stick arms. She got up and he patted her ass. She walked to the bar.

"Congressman," Mundy corrected.

"What the fuck ever," Fat Al said. His face came closer, a balloon floating toward Mundy out of the red-tinted darkness. He crossed his arms in a puddle of beer and mashed cigarette butts. Two white, flabby logs, a smudged tattoo of what seemed to Mundy to be a tongue on his right shoulder. He rested his chin on his arms. The rank smell was overpowering: Fat Al was wearing a sleeveless black T-shirt, wild tufts of coarse black hair bristling out, mashed onto the puddle on the table. Mundy had the impression that the man was silently consuming the puddle on the table through his follicles. He felt nauseous. Fat Al sat up and drew back. Mundy wondered if he had seen his reaction.

The girl came back and put a plate down in front of Fat Al. It was heaped with sliced fruit, mangoes and papayas. Dark pegs of what seemed to be small sausages and withered green hot peppers were stuck here and there in the fruit. The girl sat back down on Fat Al's leg. "I'm on a diet," he explained, digging in. "Help yourself." He put a hand on his chest, burped. "Tell you what, senator," he said again, "I got a story for you. Like this was a whatchamacallit . . . committee and I'm testifying. It's about our training. See there was this talk we had before we left? How we were the representatives of the country? Guy who gave it was this big staff sergeant, guy was like a father to us, had three tours over there. All the time he talks, he's holding a cute bunny rabbit, cuddling it in his arms." Fat Al cuddled the girl, demonstrating. "You know how it is, big tough guy, little helpless cute thing." He pinched the girl and she swore at him—Mundy presumed it swearing—in Thai. "Poignant, right? Then as soon as the speech is done, he puts the rabbit's head in his mouth, stop me if you've heard this, and he tears it off, like twisting his face to one side.

I mean, his face, not the rabbit's. The rabbit's head he spits out at the front row, tears the body to pieces with his teeth. Throws the pieces at us. Then he asked if there were any questions."

Fat Al picked up a piece of papaya and bit into it, tearing it with his teeth, twisting his head to one side abruptly, grinning at Mundy. Pieces of the red, meaty fruit dangled from his mouth, held by fibers. Juice spilled down his chin.

Mundy wasn't sure how to respond.

"Ask not," Helicopter Harry whirled a finger, his girl giggling, looking at Mundy from half-lidded eyes, "what your bunny can do for you. Now that story, Al, I mean, I grasp its universal meaning, but was it from a particular situation in your life? Or did you, let's say, sandbag it? Was it kind of a metaphor?"

"What kind of whore?"

"How about this," Helicopter Harry said. "Suppose you change it a little? A twist here, a turn there. Add an element of the unexpected. Say instead of a rabbit, a man. He stands up there, the famous Beret sergeant, petting the famous cute bunny, but then he drops it, digs his fingers in and to the astonishment of the class, sitting there, waiting for the apocryphal moment, he rips his own chest apart. Throws his own steaming heart out to them. Liver. Kidneys. Unravels his intestines and draws them out like he's pulling out a hose." Fat Al nodded, giggled. "What a show. Then, see, he dies."

"Sounds good to me." Fat Al belched. "Sure thing, Helicopter Harry." The girl was licking the juice on his chin. Mundy felt a wetness on his own cheek; his girl had turned her face and was licking it. He felt a stirring in his loins, somewhere under his disgust or maybe part of it. Chuckie's-in-Love and his girl were making out passionately. She wore yellow shorts and a black T-shirt. A red button with the number 72 was pinned on it. Chuckie's-in-Love started to nibble at the button. He raised his face. "Tell him about raping the hootch and burning the peasant," he said. "Tell him about the famous exploding shoeshine boy." He kissed the button. "I love you, seventy-two," he whispered hoarsely. "Let's get a hat."

"That's a term," Helicopter Harry explained earnestly to Congressman Mundy, "from the war."

Chuckie's-in-Love and 72 got up and left.

"Look, I'm sorry if I offended you with my choice of words," Mundy said. He spread his hands. The gesture caused the girl to sink down deeper in his lap. She turned her face up and smiled at him, her eyes widening mockingly. "I didn't mean to be patronizing." He looked at her. Epicanthic folds, he thought. It was amazing. He'd had an affair once, with a Vietnamese woman named Lily Minh in Washington, but besides her (and he found now that Lily's face was sliding into the mass) he really, literally, couldn't tell the difference between them. He was once quoted in an article—a reporter had asked him how he could ask for greater restrictions on immigration from Southeast Asia when so many people were dying in Cambodia (Kampuchea, the reporter had said)—as saying that Asians didn't feel the same way about dying as we did, since the individual wasn't important to them. It had been the wrong thing to say; he hadn't known the viciousness of the media then. But he still felt it true. "What's your name?" he asked.

The girl said something he couldn't understand.

"That's Velcro," Fat Al said.

"Why Velcro?"

"Show him, honey."

She did.

"How is that possible?" he asked. Helicopter Harry shrugged. "I didn't mean," Mundy said to him, "to co-opt your experience."

"Senator," Helicopter Harry said, "it's all yours."

"Congressman."

"What the fuck ever," Fat Al said, looking up from his feeding.

"The question I have," Helicopter Harry said, "is what you want us to do now?"

Mundy looked at the girl on Helicopter Harry's lap, her face tilted to one side in question, just as Helicopter Harry's was.

"They no speeka da Engleesh," Fat Al said.

"I told you, I particularly want vets involved in this operation. There's a real chance—"

"Where and when?" Helicopter Harry interrupted.

"How much?" Fat Al asked.

Mundy told them. They didn't say anything.

"Loman's going to meet some people who, there's a very good chance, have information on live MIAs," Mundy said. "I know you've gathered that. Once he reconnoiters, he will radio us, using a frequency we've given him. We'll then proceed to the LZ."

"You mean we'll actually vertically envelop?" Helicopter Harry said. "We'll do a real CA in an actual LZ?"

"It'll be great," Fat Al said. "We'll be an expeditionary force. That's why you want us vets, right? We've been to the edge and the edge is us. You can take the boy off the edge, but you can't take the edge out of the boy. There it is. It don't mean nothin'. That's why we love it so. We can use double-negatives. We can do anything we want. Then we go back to the World. It's numbah one." A frown crossed his face. He glared at Mundy. "What you mean, 'co-opt'? You mean the words? Where'd you get 'em? You steal 'em? You eat 'em? You a low-down word thief? A hucking metaphor?"

"Listen," Mundy said.

"How about this?" Fat Al said. "You know what bugged me, I was in the States? These billboards I seen, driving down the highway. What we do, we get together like you say, we rescue these MIAs, lean, bearded bitter guys, and we get together this little troop of scruffy vets, all experts in one sense or the other. Tunnels, demolition, PR. Then we bring 'em back to the U.S. of A. Then we form a team. We all get a bus. We chug along, see these billboards with the little evil Mexican guy painted on them? Serape, sombrero, moustache, this little evil mocking guy, like a Charlie in disguise. All these evil, jokey racist warnings on the signs. Like ethnic insults. Wetback Inn, fifty miles. Chili Today, Hot Tamale. If God Didn't Want You to Eat It, Why Did He Make It Look Like a Taco? They get pissed off at the injustice of it all, wire all the signs with plastique, blow 'em all up at once. Rush on. Then they come to this theme park, this, like, model village. War World. Hootches, waterbuff and all. Acres of jungle, booby-trapped trails. Bring the kids. Real refugees play Charlie. Real vets are point for groups of tourists. The road in, it got these little wood cut-outs on the side, little Charlies, like the little Mexican dude on the billboards. Hats, black pj's, tire sandals; only they got signs instead of weapons. Jokey sayings. Trespassers Will Be Traumatized. Do Not Roll Down Your Windows. Do Not Attempt to Relate to the Inhabitants. Tourists go through, get the whole experience in an afternoon. Trip-wire trails. Kids with booby-trapped shoeshine boxes. Ingratitude. They get mad. They get to burn down a hootch. Then they stop at the gift shop. Get a T-shirt. The MIAs look around. They can't fucking believe it. This is what they came back to? They freak. They blow away the people for real. They mine the buildings and secret tunnels where the machinery is. They blow the shit out of the place. Huge body count, dead tourists everywhere. Church groups, Japs, family dogs, Latin American death squads and their families with videocameras, up on vacation. They waste 'em all. Then they find this secret place where all the stolen words were taken. These bamboo cages that they got the missing words in. They free 'em. They take 'em all back."

He looked at Mundy as if waiting for him to say something.

"Are you Hispanic?" Mundy asked.

"Am I Hispanic?" Fat Al said. "I love you, senator."

Helicopter Harry and all the girls were laughing, the noise throbbing in Mundy's head. He looked at them, feeling thick and drunk. Sitting outside the language of men.

YOKTHE PWE

The thirty-seven royal nats are:

Thagyamin, the king
The Lord of the Great Mountain
Princess Golden Face
Lady Golden Sides
Lady Three-fold Beautiful
Small Flute Lady
The Brown Lord of the South
The White Lord of the North
White Umbrella Lord
His Royal Mother
Lord Pareim-ma
Old Base Gold
Young Base Gold
Lord Grandfather of Mandalay
Lord Bandy Legs
Old Banyan Tree Man
Lord Sithu
Young Lord of the Swing

Valiant Lord Kyaw Swa
Captain Aung Swa
Royal Cadet
Lady Golden Words
Lord Five Elephants
Lord King, Master of Justice
Maung Po Tu
Queen of the Western Palace
Master of White Elephants
Lady Bent
Golden Nawrahta
Valiant Lord Aung Din
Lord White
Lord Novice
Tabinshweti
Lady of the North
Lord Minh Kaung
Royal Secretary
The King of Chiengmai

Only four other passengers besides Loman, Charlene, and Usama were on the UBA flight. Loman had one side of the aisle for himself. Two young men in checkered *longyis*, the Burmese sarongs, embroidered Shan bags slung over their shoulders, sat across the aisle from him and talked softly as they rolled balls of rice and pork from the palm leaf–wrapped parcels in their laps. Behind them was an elderly Burmese woman so plump that the skin of her face, under the paste of *thanaka*-leaf powder, seemed pumped up smooth and taut as a balloon. She sat stiffly, her hand continually crabbing up to inventory her jewelry: uncultured pearl earrings set in silver, a ruby and star sapphire necklace. Charlene and Usama sat after her, then a florid-faced white man who joked with the flight attendant in booming, British-accented Burmese. As soon as the plane was airborne, the attendant sat down, extracted her own palm-wrapped packet from under the seat, and began scooping rice into her mouth as if stocking for a famine.

Loman waited until she had finished, then signaled to her and ordered a bourbon. She smiled and brought him a beer.

Being physically on the airplane didn't make what he was doing seem any more real to him. He ran a litany of figures through his mind again as if to reassure himself that this trip was anchored in mature motivations. Charlene and Usama had offered $10,000 or a share in the profits of the MIA film. He had taken the money. Half of it was already in the Naga Queen's. Mundy—or rather Weyland—was paying $25,000 plus expenses, and Loman had bargained him up another $5,000, which he was carrying on him in traveler's checks. The entire trip shouldn't take more than two weeks. It was good money for being little more than a messenger and a tour guide. It would keep the bar afloat.

He drank the beer and looked out the window, trying to see the ocean. The plane was above the clouds.

Up the aisle, Charlene and Usama were dressed in his-and-her khaki safari suits. They didn't look happy. Loman wasn't sure if they had bought the necessity of going north through Burma instead of Thailand. Usama, he saw, was taking apart his camera and putting it together like a soldier field-stripping a weapon. When Loman had told Charlene, Usama had filmed the exchange between them, bringing his lens up close to her face, so that Loman suddenly saw her as if through the viewfinder, focusing in and out: a line of sweat springing to her forehead, her eyes going sleepy and disinterested.

"Look, you hired me for what I know," Loman had said. "If you'd rather do it on your own, go north your own way, that's still your option." He didn't mention Aung Khin to them.

"What have you done to us, Yank?" Charlene had said.

Loman found her words strange. But the two of them had gone along with it. They believed in their film. It was what they had instead of a bar.

He thought about Mundy, waiting for him in Bangkok to

send word about the missing. Waiting for his defining moment. He finished his beer. The clouds outside boiled into suggestive, vaguely menacing shapes. It was near sunset. The plane began its descent to Mingalon airport. A jade landscape pinned flat by the spires of golden pagodas burned beneath the wing, like a dream that should have been gone when he turned to look. A cleaner, greener land.

He and Charlene and Usama were the last off the plane. Two men dressed identically in khaki short-sleeved shirts, black trousers, and flip-flops came up next to Loman. They each had short-cropped black hair and were stocky, the muscles in their brown arms accentuated by the constricting elastic of their sleeves. They looked like brothers, but it was the resemblance gained by men who share a profession, Loman thought.

"Welcome to Myanmar, Mr. Loman," one said. The other man put his hand over Usama's lens and pulled the camera down. He smiled but kept his hand firmly over the lens.

The first man tapped sharply on the customs counter. The agent handed him their passports.

"Our transportation is outside, Mr. Loman."

"Whither he goest, mate," Charlene said, "we're along for the ride."

"Yes you are," the man said.

A dusty brown Mercedes was parked in front of the terminal. The man who hadn't spoken opened the back door for Loman and smiled as he had smiled when he pushed down Usama's camera. Loman looked at the dark space inside.

"You won't be harmed," the other man said softly.

"Yes we are," Charlene said.

"We're only taking you to your hotel. You'll wait there. Someone will come for you; someone to take you north."

■ ■ ■

The Inya Lake Hotel was built to imitate a form of concrete and glass Western luxury, but form hadn't been enough to hold it together. Its paint was peeling, its plaster was wet and cracked. The conditioned air smelled moldy. There weren't many guests, but there seemed to be a wedding reception in the dining area. Loman glimpsed an abundance of Prisoner of Zenda military uniforms, sunbursts of rubies, diamonds, sapphires, gold, a frenzy of wearable luxury so that the guests seemed like looters in the ruins. He went to his room. The vinyl shower curtain in the bathroom was heavy with black mold. His bed had been neatly made, but the sheets were musty and slightly stiff, apparently unchanged from the last guest. He lay on it anyway.

His mind kept working on Weyland and Mundy and he couldn't sleep. Charlene and Usama were next door. He drifted off to the moans coming through the thin wall.

He woke, not sure how long he had been out, but suddenly full of a restless energy that drove him out of the room and down to the lobby. The wedding was over. The reception hall was almost empty, except for a few French tourists and a group of young Burmese in tennis outfits. They looked at Loman and the other foreigners, a raw hunger in their eyes that made him turn away. Shrill bursts of embarrassed laughter exploded from the people in the group, as if they had just realized they were the victims of an unpleasant joke.

Loman went to the bar. There was no bourbon, so he drank cheap scotch at an inflated price. He told the bartender he owned a bar in Bangkok. The man leaned over the counter and asked for a job, whispering that he would sneak over the border if Loman would guarantee it. A tall, thin man wearing a longyi and a checkered Western shirt sat on the next chair.

He wore a name tag with the word *Manager* on it in English, and Burmese letters underneath. He said he had been educated in the States and asked Loman how he liked the condition of the hotel.

"There's no paint," the man said. The same laugh Loman had heard in the lobby burst from his lips. "No paint, no point, isn't it? But I do have requisition forms." He laughed shrilly. "At least the hotel will never be short of toilet paper, isn't it? Do you think you'd enjoy that? As a guest? I'm taking a market survey. It's one of the skills I picked up in the States that I've found so useful here."

He showed Loman pictures of his wife, an architect who had stayed in America when his student visa had expired; he was desperate to rejoin her. In the pictures, she was standing in front of a townhouse in Burke, Virginia, beckoning with her hands, a slightly mocking smile on her lips. The door behind her was closed.

An older man sat down on the other side of Loman and looked at the pictures also. He smiled at Loman.

"One of our more famous monks said that if one looks at beautiful things constantly, one will get tired, and suffering, probably in the form of disgust, will set in."

"It hasn't," Loman said, "been one of my problems." The man wore the turbanlike traditional Burmese headgear, the *gaung-baung*, and a silk round-collared long-sleeved jacket. His deep brown face was socketed with shadow, his eyes liquid and deep. The manager looked at him and his face went blank. He sat very still.

The older man kept smiling at Loman. "Where are you visiting us from?"

"Thailand."

"Ah. But you are American."

"Yes."

The hotel manager was slowly drawing the photograph of his wife back to him, across the countertop, as if cautiously pulling it away from a trap.

"And what do you think of Myanmar?" the man said.

"I've only been here a few hours."

"But this isn't your first trip," the man said casually.

Loman took another drink.

The man said, "Now if I were a tourist, I'd be interested in the story of the Maha Gandha bell. Do you know it? I'll tell it to you. It was cast some two centuries ago, of bronze, and it weighs, I think it is twenty tons."

"Twenty-three," the manager said eagerly.

"Ah. Thank you so much. When the British were here, they tried to take it to London, all twenty-three," he nodded to the manager, "tons, but it sank to the bottom of the Irrawaddy when they attempted to float it across, and they couldn't raise it again, no matter how they tried. Their technology was inadequate. They couldn't get the right materials. Our people told them that if they promised to return the bell to the pagoda, we would raise it. The British agreed. They believed we would fail. But it was our bell. We simply sent divers down with bamboo tubes, tied them one by one to the bell until it floated up. Our bell, our way."

Loman was tired of cryptic messages. "It's funny how hanging on to a culture is so often an excuse for repressing your own people, not to mention a lack of goods and services," he said, raising his scotch.

The man looked into his eyes. "Myanmar and Thailand are mirrors to each other, Mr. Loman." He unsheathed his knowledge of Loman's name with deliberation. "Each stares into a bad choice."

"What are the choices?" Loman asked.

"Whoring or deprivation."

Loman raised his drink and toasted his two old friends. He

looked into the mirror. Trung, his old reflection, smiled his mocking smile. Loman toasted him too.

The manager excused himself and left hastily.

"Then of course there are those responsible for both choices, Mr. Loman. Often they give themselves missions, tasks of merit, to make themselves feel better."

Loman finished his drink. "In a world of whores and beggars, the one-eyed pimp is king," he said. "See, I'm just this country boy, chief. What are you getting at?"

"Do you know the word *anandeh*?" the old man said.

"I've heard it. I was never sure what it meant." Actually, he did, but he figured the old man was going to tell him anyway.

"It's hard to translate. Roughly it has to do with convincing a person of the futility of his desires, but doing so without a painfully direct confrontation, without causing the person to become an enemy."

Loman looked interested. "I'd say more a painful unwillingness to define a situation completely, in case one might offend another's intelligence. But I'm this simple bar owner. So why don't you spell it out for me."

The old man laughed. "As you said, just a country boy. And I like your country, Mr. Loman. I visited there, even as you have come to me. I enjoyed particularly driving through the space of it. Wherever I went, your friendly people would ask me where I was from, and when I said: 'Burma,' they wouldn't know where that was. That made me deeply happy. I'm sure if I had said I was from Vietnam or Cambodia, they would have known immediately where those places were. Even if I had said Thailand, they would have known."

Loman kept up his expression of interest. "Tell me, did this really happen? Or is this one of those stories that has a hidden moral?"

The man tapped sharply on the bar. The bartender brought

him a tall gin and tonic. He kept his face blank and didn't make eye contact with either Loman or the old man.

"I can't stop you, Mr. Loman, from touring my country. The ally your employer has chosen has too many allies of his own. Please understand me, I do like your people. They are restless with the need to do good, to gain merit, so much so that often the consequences of striving to be loved are not fully examined. You, I think, understand this. I have other friends in your country too who understand also, who told me that you would be coming. I would appreciate if if you would let the man you represent know this, Mr. Loman."

"I have no idea what you're talking about."

The man smiled at Loman. *Anandeh.*

Loman walked out of the hotel. The traffic was sparse. There were some new Japanese cars, but many of the others looked like they had escaped from his childhood. He saw an old Nash Rambler, a '49 Mercury, and a '57 Chevy moving like hallucinations next to jitneys and World War II Japanese buses and bullock-drawn carts. He walked under jacaranda trees that seemed thickenings of the darkness, past decaying examples of British colonial architecture, teak houses on stilts, their high-peaked roofs elaborately carved and showing above the parting silhouettes of palm fronds like the prows of ships. The air was fragrant with sandalwood and woodsmoke. Slim, long-fingered men and women in *longyis* glided by in the darkness gathered under the umbrella spreads of the peepul and banyan trees, their faces half-lit by fires from the braziers. Loman felt an undefinable, amnesiac's ache, like the knowledge of a loss whose details he couldn't remember.

He sat at a curbside bench and drank sugarcane juice. It was squeezed from stalks of cane by a wooden roller device that reminded him of the old-fashioned wringer his mother had had on the washing machine out on the front porch. The Burmese sitting and drinking stared at him and smiled whenever they made eye contact. A boy with a long, pocked face sat down next to Loman, straddling the chair backward, his arms over the backrest as if to get a better view.

"Are you British?"

"American."

"Do you mind if we speak? I need to practice my English."

The boy reached across, took the fabric of Loman's sleeve between his fingers, rubbed it gently and sighed.

"Your English is good."

"BBC," the boy said, then added, "VOA," as if not to offend Loman's nationality. "I want to go to America."

"Why?"

"I can't get work here."

"There are people in America who can't get work."

The boy laughed politely.

"Whoring or deprivation," Loman said.

A tall woman in a formal silk *longyi* and a long-sleeved jacket that glittered with silver threads came up to the vendor and ordered a drink. She looked resplendent and incongruous in the dust under the trees. She sipped the drink delicately and looked at Loman with indifference. The vendor, an old man with three rotting teeth in his mouth, said something and she smiled, the smile opening her face with sudden surprise, like a flower finding sun. It closed again when she looked back at Loman, her eyes sliding off his flesh as if its color repulsed her. Unselfconsciously, she loosened the waist on her *longyi*, held it out from her body, then tightened it, like someone tightening a towel. Loman, staring at the graceful movement, felt his throat constrict, echoing the same motion. This time the woman didn't avoid his stare. As if she were performing a trick, her face transformed into the face of the woman behind the counter in the Hotel Miami. Loman's hair bristled. He got up and started toward her. She turned, looked over her shoulder, and smiled, as she had smiled at him in the darkness of the hallway.

A white-coated houseboy (did they still dare to call them that?) passed, and Weyland snatched a drink from his tray. He saw that he was the only person standing by himself. Several dips glanced at him uneasily: he was a nation of uncertain alliance. The layered, nuanced chatter around him, references within references, the knowledgeable laughter, the significant glances, all the riffs and shuffles brought him back. He'd always despised embassy receptions, but the memory of his distaste woke a kind of nostalgia in him now. Weyland looked at his congressman, standing next to the ambassador and his wife; they were being professionally gracious and witty to a small sycophantic cluster of second secretaries and spouses. He had insisted Mundy come to the reception. The boys had given him a hard time; he needed to be reassured about himself, have others around who would tell him who he was. It had been the right choice. Mundy looked relieved and relaxed here, at home in the familiar patterns of the party.

Weyland brought the glass up, almost to his lips, allowing himself to imagine the first, smooth bite of the scotch, the way he would hold it in his mouth before he swallowed, the warmth it would leave in his throat and chest. He put the whiskey down.

He'd been assessing Mundy, he realized, thinking of him in terms he would use in a report on an agent he was running, if he still did reports: what motivated him, what was the picture of himself he wanted to have? It was another kind of nostalgia. He'd missed the art of it. Art imposing order on the chaos of life.

"Art," Tom Pritchard said, walking across the parquet teak floor as if his outstretched hand was pulling him. Weyland shook it, touched the cold, slightly wet flesth of the past. Pritchard had once been the head of a Country Team with which he'd worked.

"I hardly know what to say," Tom Pritchard said.

"What can you say to the dead?"

Pritchard brought up his glass and nodded at Weyland's glass, sitting on the table. Weyland picked it up. "The dead," he said.

He put the whiskey down, untouched.

The laughter from the group around the ambassador grew louder.

"Art," Pritchard said again, shaking his head. "The wind blew, the shit flew, and here stands Art Weyland." He sighed. "Do we retire to the basement, hook your testes up to a field telephone, and call for some answers?" He smiled to show it was possibly a joke.

Weyland looked around the room again. "Sandy with you?"

"The divorce became final last month."

Weyland nodded brightly as if Pritchard had given the correct answer.

Pritchard put on a morose look. "Elliott Mundy," he said.

Weyland smiled at him.

"All the money the boy's got behind him, who'd a thunk he needed you. Charlie Greaves, Paul D. Lukas, the billionaire club MIA bunch. You find, we fund. You on with that, Art? You grunion hunting MIAs with the congressfella?"

Weyland kept smiling.

"Elliott Mundy," Pritchard said again. "Somehow I can't find the words."

"If I remember, the word we used to use was 'challenging.'"

Pritchard chuckled. "This year it's 'paradigm.' Last year it was 'module.' I never learn them in time. That's why they wouldn't let me stay in Langley. Incidentally, that's why Sandy left."

"Because you didn't have the right words?"

"It was because I didn't stay at Langley," Pritchard said patiently. "Our last posting was Nigeria. She refused to go abroad again. WAWA."

"West Africa Wins Again." Weyland nodded.

"The camel's back, as it were, broke when one of the legs on the table she used as a desk broke. She was fond of that table; she'd used it since Georgetown. Instead of a new desk, she asked Mr. Carpenter to put on a new leg. Match it up. Mr. Carpenter did, and of course he made it exactly the length of the broken leg. It was a new broken leg. WAWA."

There was a kind of nostalgia in doing this dance too, Weyland thought. The dance of not-so-oblique warnings and clumsy analogies: Weyland had been involved in a failed attempt to get a particular African politician he'd cultivated into power. "I liked Africa," he said.

"And Asia can be fun too, can't it?" Pritchard wagged a finger at Weyland. "Art, we're watching you. You're not Mr. Spy anymore."

"I'm Mr. Consultant. I do it because people didn't want me around. I was an embarrassment. I kept using words that were no longer current." He looked around, then whispered furtively, "Veetnam."

"Hush, now," Pritchard said. "The children will hear. There are ladies present."

"I know. I'm not to remind anyone. I'm to be Missing."

Pritchard was staring at him. "Art, you're not going to make it all better, are you? You and the boy wonder? We know what he's into, Mr. Congressperson. But the Us stories, all the MIA stories, are just a men's magazine fantasy." He squinted at Weyland as if something had just occurred to him. "Or you and I still on the same team and nobody thought poor old Pritch needed to know? Compartments within boxes, is that it? I touch the elephant's trunk, you got hold of its dick? Everything deniable, the president never even knew you were born, and besides he wasn't even there when he talked to you."

"We're just here on a tour, Pritch, the congressman and I. A tour of post-Veetnam Asia."

Pritchard didn't look relieved. "You keep your boy out of mischief. You hear? And you stay away from Aung Khin." He threw the name out like his last card.

"Who?"

"Wireless Willy," Pritchard said, using Weyland's old cover name for Khin. "He still have fear of the airwaves?"

"I wouldn't know. Tell me something, Pritch."

"What's that?"

"Men's magazines. They still have those?"

"Keep your boy away," Pritchard said again. "The sign is hung out. True believers not welcome."

Weyland looked over at his congressman.

"It's not that I'm unsympathetic," Pritchard said. "But you above all should understand the present situation."

If he were writing a report of his reasons for choosing

Mundy, what would he say? How would he assess the asset? He remembered when Mundy had first come to his attention, it must have been around 1984. The congressman had been depressed that the world seemed to have shifted under his feet. He'd thought he had made the right move by not going to the war when he had been of an age to go.

"The unqualified doing the unnecessary in the name of the ungrateful," Pritchard said. "As usual."

But that year the war came back to haunt Mundy like a flashback from an experience he'd never even had. Its unfinished business suddenly seemed everywhere, glowing larger than life on movie screens, asking him for recompense from behind the cash registers in 7-Elevens in his home district. That year the war appeared in his life like the missing in the form of a Vietnam veteran named Robert Travers who challenged him for his seat. Travers was a man Mundy had known, and discounted, years before. He had gone to marine OCS in the same year Mundy had used the excuse of a tennis injury to get a draft deferment and go to law school. Not only had Travers been decorated, he'd been mutilated: shrapnel had disfigured his face, torn off his left arm, and severed his spine. He campaigned in his wheelchair. Although Mundy refused to debate him, Travers came to every forum and rally, presenting his torn body like a bill paid for Mundy's failure to show up.

"Policy has become a kind of enforced impotence. Enforced by the media and the professoriat, more than by us. The only politically correct history is self-criticism," Pritchard said.

Underfunded and underconnected, Travers never had a chance. But Mundy had felt accused, vulnerable to punishment for a failure to act that he hadn't even considered a sin. He soothed himself with acts of contrition.

"*We are baaad, we are bad, we are bad, bad, bad, yes the best of us is no damn good,*" Pritchard sang.

He became the vets' best friend, pushing for extended benefits, sponsoring memorials. He vehemently opposed normalization of relations with Vietnam until the MIA issue was cleared up, a stance which brought him favorable notice from the POW/MIA lobby.

"Better stay home," Pritchard said. "Or sew a Canadian maple leaf on all the flags at all the embassies, so we won't get our ass kicked."

He initiated and chaired a congressional committee on MIAs.

Weyland, looking for a man, had sensed a pattern.

"Desert One. Beirut. We go out in it, we get dead."

What was the picture of himself he wanted to have? Weyland had gotten to Mundy through a Vietnamese woman named Lily Minh. He'd made sure she and Mundy were both at MIA fund-raisers and rallies; he put her into Mundy's life; she did the same for him. Lily's father, a former prime minister, had been one of Weyland's assets; he'd known her since she was a little girl. She had been glad to do him a favor.

"You know how it is, Art," Pritchard eyed him uneasily. "We hang on during this swing of the pendulum as always. But the decade is ending. This too will pass. Then we come back. Us grown-ups."

Mundy encased himself in her, the flesh of Vietnam. To her own amusement, Lily, who understood Mundy's solipsism perfectly, told Weyland that during sex, staring unblinking into Mundy's eyes, she saw the world she came from flicker like frames in a burning film, shrink or elongate, change at a blink or a mood from forests to lakes, from huts to castles. Embracing Mundy's pale body, Lily came to feel that her orgasms were intellectual before they were physical: she'd come to America to escape history and consequences and in Mundy she saw the living possibility. Mundy was an immigrant's, a war refugee's, dream; he was, she told Weyland, an ocean between herself and the world.

"I sympathize," Pritchard said. "I even envy you. Your freedom to act in the world. But what can I say?"

Weyland picked up his glass again and raised it in the direction of Elliott Mundy. The untouched whiskey in it caught the soft light of the room and seemed to shimmer with possibility, with latent power.

Loman was getting tired of this woman disappearing around corners. He raced after her, weaving, pushing. He broke through next to her.

The great golden bell-shape of a temple stupa materialized in front of his eyes, a light that had been switched on when the darkness came.

"Shwedagon," Kitty said.

She moved ahead when he tried to come to her side, but waved him to follow her. They entered a walkway, roofed with overlapping, serpentine scales that angled up to the Shwedagon. He hurried after her to the foot of the stairs; if he took his eyes off her she would cease to exist.

Stalls selling flowers, incense, carved sandalwood saints, the packets of gold leaf that worshipers would stick on the side of the stupa, lined the walkway. A group of chattering schoolgirls, their cheeks so white with fresh thanaka powder they looked to Loman like mimes playing schoolgirls, clattered down the steps. Each was carrying a straw broom: they were gaining merit by cleaning the temple platform. Kitty gestured to the chinthe, the half-lion, half-griffin guarding the foot of the stairs, and smiled.

"He's here to make sure that visitors remove their shoes and socks."

Loman took them off. They walked barefoot as children and side by side now up the stairs. Teak beams, blackened with age, showed through the sides of the walls in places, like exposed bones. There was no noise, except for the faint sound of chanting, drifting down to them in the tunnel. They stepped out onto the central platform. The marble was cool under his feet. A bell rang, its sound moving in waves through the quilted hush. The chanting of monks reverberated out from the ring, into the drone of her voice. The *stupa* of the Shwedagon that he saw above them, she said, was 326 feet high and was covered by 8,688 slabs of solid gold and was built to contain 8 hairs of the last Buddha. The *hti*, the upside-down umbrella sticking out just below the point of the spire, was made of 7 gold plates and 420 silver bells and was there to catch any of the more than 5,000 diamonds or the more than 2,300 topazes, sapphires, and rubies, or the one emerald embedded above it, should they fall.

"Are you a tour guide?"

How else, she asked him, would a good Burmese girl be seen walking alone with a Western man, except as a tour guide?

They walked under a pillar with a *hintha*, a sacred bird figure sitting on top. They were moving toward the center. Women were pasting gold leaf on the base of the stupa. A small temple nested to one side, the standing Buddha in the *tazaung* niche inside, staring calmly at Loman, his palm upraised as if he wanted Loman to stare into it and see his future.

"Where did you take me last time, tour guide?" he asked. "What did you do to me?"

She said, looking at the Buddha, "The position he is standing in is called the *Abhaya Mudra*. It evokes protection and tranquillity, but at another level reminds us of danger, an attempt to assassinate the Buddha. Don't you remember what happened?"

"No. Only that you stuck your fingers into my head and stirred up shit that's still floating around." He took her arm. "Tell me."

She broke free of him, as easily as if she were only drifting down corridors in his mind.

The circular base of the *stupa*, its curved flank glowing above them, rested on a gradated series of octagonal terraces. On the next level up Loman saw a group of monks sitting cross-legged on the ledge, their hands spread, their eyes closed. Silence emanated from them like the wavering of heat in air, as forceful and as peaceful as the chanting all around them. Kitty sat on a small marble bench. He sat next to her.

"I'm sorry for what happened," she said. "But it was necessary to slow you down. And you were not harmed."

"What did we do in your room?" he insisted.

She grimaced. "You never came to my room, Mr. Loman. Your face frightened me. You came after me until the drug hit you, and then you fell. We put you in a car and brought you back to the city."

"I don't believe you."

"Near the northern stairway," Kitty said, "there's a tank where King Anawrahta's general washed the blood off his sword before he came to pray."

"You have no idea," Loman said, "how tired I am of being fucked around with."

She nodded, squinting into the darkness, then speaking to it, so softly he had to move closer to her to hear.

"In our belief, Loman, in the center of the world is Mount Meru. To its south is our continent, which is called Jambudipa. It is a place of misery and suffering. It is a place where people are fucked around with. It is not like the northern continent where clothing and an abundance of food, already cooked, are simply plucked by the fortunate inhabitants from the trees, where the inhabitants live to be one thousand years old, where there is no suffering."

"Lady," Loman said, "I live here."

"Why are you so angry at me?"

To his surprise, Loman said: "Because I don't want to be simplified and dismissed by you."

Their stares held for a moment. "Why on earth do you care?" she said.

"Who are you?" he said. "What do you do in Bangkok, at the Hotel Miami?"

She laughed. "I'm simplified and dismissed. Isn't what I'm doing here more important?"

"Here you're a tour guide. You brought me to a pagoda. Okay, I'm the novice *pongyi*, you the wise *sayadaw*. Enlighten me."

"I hope to do that. I came to Rangoon to tell you what you have been doing and what you must do."

"Thank God," Loman said sincerely.

"You've been acting out an illusion."

"Oh hell," Loman said, waving at the monks, "that's what they all say."

"Aung Khin's business is illusion," she said, speaking as if the words had been thought out many times before, her speech chanted like a monk's prayer she would now recite to him in sequence, no matter what he said. "He supplies the illusions of your people."

"Khin sells opium and heroin. Both are real enough."

"Khin sells only number four, the purest of illusions."

"How about you?" Loman said. "What are you selling today?"

"I don't sell. I'm bought."

"Sweet Jesus," Loman said in exasperation. He looked up. A monk looked down at him, reproachfully, he thought.

"No, not sweet Jesus nor even Lord Buddha, Loman. Just Aung Khin. The Hotel Miami is his, I keep it for him. That's the first step in your enlightenment. Yes, to answer the question you're going to ask: he could easily have met Mundy there. He didn't want to. But it is a place for him to come when he is in Bangkok: for meetings, for planning, for business, for the gathering of information, for the housing of couriers. I arrange these things for him, in the Hotel Miami and in a similar place I keep for him in Chiang Mai. I do other things for him, when he comes to these places. Do you want to know what they are? I can't tell you what you did in the Hotel Miami, but I can tell you what Aung Khin does with me. Would that satisfy the other question in your eyes?"

"I don't want to know."

She laughed incredulously. "Why not? What do you think I am?" She held up her hand, imitating the gesture of the Buddha. "I'm telling you what I do so you will understand how I know about Mundy and his plans. Aung Khin also talks to me, Loman. It seems to be one of his other needs."

Loman stared at her. "What are you?"

"A hole in the earth for secrets." A bell rang, the sound stirring into her voice. "Once upon a time," she said hollowly, "there was a little girl who lived in a palace made of white poppies in a kingdom far to the north."

She closed her eyes and shook her head rapidly, as if clearing whatever had come into it. A strand of black hair came loose. Loman stared at it with a sense of voyeurism, as if it were the physical representation of some secret spilling from her. She opened her eyes and stared into his. He shuddered.

"What are you?" he repeated.

"Once I was a student. I learned things. I received an education. I graduated and went to the jungle. It's not an unusual story in my generation."

"Jesus," Loman said.

"No," she said. "Taksin."

"You just told me you work for Aung Khin. Are they the same person?"

"We hope not," she said.

"Then what?"

"I told you, Aung Khin talks to me. But Taksin listens."

Loman closed his eyes. "Okay," he said, the novice monk translating the obscure Pali text his teacher chanted into the language of the world. "You were a student; after the soldiers shot up the democracy demonstrations, you went north, joined Taksin's guerrillas, is that right? And now you run an intelligence and logistics operation for Khin in the Hotel Miami, but actually you spy on him for Taksin. You understand where I might have a little trouble with this?"

"There isn't time for me to explain more completely, Loman. Listen to me. Khin is threatened by Taksin. He is trying to exterminate us. He'll use Mundy to do it."

"How?"

"There isn't time for you to know everything."

"What do you want?"

She looked surprised. "You must go to Taksin, not Aung Khin," she said, as if it were obvious.

"Why?"

"Loman, you have to. The missing are with Taksin," she said desperately. "Not with Aung Khin. You'll find them there." Loman half-rose. There was a stir in the crowd of worshipers, a ripple moving through it. He thought he saw a man pointing a camera, Usama. The realization struck him like a meditational stage, the insight that sees suddenly the unity of cause and effect. "Charlene and Usama," he said. They'd put the idea of Taksin into his head. "They're yours," he said.

She sighed. "They were sympathizers, with the movement; they help us. Yes, we had them come to you."

Loman thought about it for a second, then cursed. "You screwed me royally, didn't you? If Khin knows about Charlene and Usama it's already finished."

"He doesn't. No more than he knows about me."

"Shit," Loman said, seeing it, the next stage on his road to enlightenment. "Okay, you knew Mundy and Weyland were coming to me—Aung Khin talks to you, like you said. Among other things. You knew Weyland arranged with Aung Khin that I'd be the go-between. So you preempted them. You tried to get me to go to Taksin with Charlene and Usama and their phony movie."

"Mundy came sooner than I thought he would," she admitted. "And their film isn't phony: having our permission to do it was their price."

"You pressured me," he said, seeing the path that had been opened for him while, like all mortals in the suffering continent of Jambudipa, he'd had the illusion of choice. "Was Krit with you? Hell, the guy who did the German, was he yours too?"

"No. He is Aung Khin's. Aung Khin wanted to be sure you would accept Mundy's offer."

It might even be true, Loman thought. There was no way he could know. Everybody wanted him to take this trip, and either way he'd been squeezed. "Why?" he said again. "Why do you want me to go to Taksin?"

"You must," she said, her eyes flitting away. "You must—to find the missing."

He threw up his hands. "Taksin," he said. "Is that his real name? Is he Burmese? Why the Thai name?"

"We all took different names in the north—to confuse authority." She fluttered her fingers at the saffron-robed monks sitting cross-legged under the roof of a small pagoda, the chanters. "Sometimes one has to give up one's name, like they do. Sometimes names can bind too tightly."

"What's your name, in the north?"

"Sadong," she whispered. He felt a chill, as though she had slipped her soul into his hands. But he wondered if even that name were real—the name she'd given him, he realized, was Thai, not Burmese—if she was still protecting something from him. Something else occurred to him.

"Why didn't you tell me all this in the Hotel Miami?"

"I didn't know who you were when you came. When I did find out, it was too late."

"When you brought me to your room."

"Loman, please. There's no time."

"Why did you come here?" he insisted. "You could have asked me through Charlene and Usama."

"You already refused them."

"Their lies didn't work, your tactic is truth. You want me to accept the revealed word and act out of faith. Hell, even if I believe you, why should I help you?"

"Because of the color of your eyes."

Loman laughed.

"Did you know that many of the demonstrations for democracy here," she said slowly, "were in front of your embassy? The soldiers the government brought into Rangoon—they used kids from other parts of the country—cursed at the demonstrators, particularly the young women, and said they wanted to copulate with the foreigners. The women cursed back at them, saying better their blue eyes than your black eyes. But when the soldiers shot into the crowds, when they clubbed young women to death in the lake, your people did nothing."

"And that surprised you?" Loman said. "Hell, I thought you said you had an education. What did you do, skip history?"

He felt a sudden wave of anger, not, to his surprise, at the way he had been manipulated, but at her, that she could give herself, soul and body, to serve a name, a flag, an idea of freedom that in the end would be bought by corpses and whoring.

"This Taksin of yours apparently finances politics with opium, just like every other Terry and the Pirates army in the Triangle," Loman said. "He's just like Khin. He's a pimp who made you a whore."

Loman saw Trung asking him if he got the joke.

"Even if that were true, why would it make you so angry, Loman?"

"I'll go to Taksin," he said.

"Good. Then you—"

He raised his hand. "I'll go if you take me."

She sat very still, looking puzzled. "Why?"

Loman didn't know how to put it; his own words had surprised him. Finally he said, "I want to save you from whoring yourself."

She looked at him in amazement. He didn't blame her. "Given your profession I find that hard to believe. Or perhaps that itself is an explanation—like the color of your eyes. But in any case, it's impossible."

"It would just be coming home," he said. Her face twitched. For a second he thought he had succeeded in moving her into his dream, an instant of hope opening in her eyes.

And closing. "I can't," she said. "I can't leave the Hotel Miami. I'm Taksin's eyes and ears."

"You got your anatomy wrong too," Loman said.

The van, an oversized Econoline, descended into a deep rift. The road flowed down to a river. They had been driving for two nights and three days and Loman was disoriented. For all he knew they were out of Burma now; the river could be the Kok or the Salween or the Mekong. The walls of the rift, thick with jungle, rose on both sides. The sky was a line of blue chewed on by the gums of a grotesquely elongated mouth. The driver, a young Burmese named Win, flashed a smile at Loman and let his eyes float contemptuously to the back seat where Charlene and Usama slept, oblivious to the country, eyes closed, camera lens capped. The inside of the van filled with a greenish underwater light that turned Win's skin to tarnished copper.

"We stop soon," he said. "Eat."

"Where are we?" Loman asked.

"Mountains."

"Thailand or Burma?"

"Mountains," Win said, as if Loman were simple. "Mountains doan care. Got teak, got elephants, got tiger. Got barking deer here, Lo-man. Human fellow goes into the jungle this place, he takes a little yellow barking dog, so the tiger eat it first." He laughed and pounded the wheel. The van swerved. Charlene cursed sleepily from the back seat. "North-south mountains," Win said. "End of the world, Lo-man."

"I have to pee," Charlene said.

Win grinned and stopped. "You wan a yellow dog, lady?" He giggled. Charlene gave him a dirty look. She slid the door open and got out, stretching. The oval leaves of teak trees pressed a weave of shadows on the yellow dirt of the narrow road. Usama reached for his camera and switched it on, then stretched also, coming to life. He pointed the lens at Charlene, who gave him the finger. He kept shooting. Win waved at the trees.

"Ladies' loo," he said. "Watch out for tigers."

Charlene gave him a disdainful look and went into the bushes. Usama followed, still filming.

They came back in a minute.

"Christ, mate," Charlene muttered. "No tiger, but something tickled me fancy."

Loman wondered if he would get a chance to talk to her alone again. Up to this point, Win had stayed with them constantly. Usama turned the camera on Loman, to get his reaction. A picture of Charles Jambeau, a French photographer Loman had once accompanied into the city of Hue, swam into his mind. The city was off-limits to GIs, which was why Loman wanted to go; they'd used the Frenchman's press pass and gone there like armed tourists. Jambeau had kept his eye glued to the camera the whole time as if seeing the country that way protected him from it. When he died in a helicopter crash three weeks after their day trip, Loman had asked if his camera had been recovered, but the medic he talked to said they couldn't even identify the photographer's teeth. He'd wondered if Jambeau had filmed his own last moments, held the camera up between himself and the land rushing up at him.

"Get that thing out of my face," he said.

"You're part of the story," Charlene said. "We paid for you."

The anger in her voice made Win turn and stare at her.

She had come into Loman's hotel room in Rangoon the night he spoke to Sadong. After he had gotten back to the hotel, he had bought three bottles of beer and went up to his room to try to sleep. He rested a bottle in a pool of sweat on his stomach and sipped. He kept dozing off into a dream that concerned a series of grotesque situations whose details he immediately forgot. The bottle in his hand kept slipping and pulling him out of the dream. In the dream, he knew that it was an important rule of behavior not to accept the reversal of structures, though he had no idea what that meant. He only knew that if he lay still long enough on the clammy sheets in his own stale sweat, the waking world would eventually make sense to him again.

Only that night it hadn't. The rules of the waking world had become as whimsical as the customs of his dreams. He thought of Kitty. Opening her *longyi*, revealing nothing, closing it, as off-limits as Hue. That night, in his hotel room, Loman had stared at the dark rectangle of the door, filling it with her shape, willing her to come to him. And the door had opened.

"Did I wake you?" Charlene had said.

"No."

She sat on the bed and stared at him.

"Is this where you offer yourself to me if I'll change my mind?"

Charlene shrugged. "Would it work?"

"I'm tired of bad movies and heartless fucking."

"The modern dilemma, mate."

"What about the missing?" he asked her. "Are they really with Taksin?"

"That's a contradiction in terms, isn't it?"

"I'm too tired for this," he said. "Why don't you go now."

Charlene rested her chin on her hand.

"You're going to hurt a lot of people."

"Any way I move," he nodded. "Same-same with you, or Sadong. The trick is to either stay still or turn a profit."

"*Kon Ahn Harm Kon Die*," she said.

Loman took a long swig. "Where the hell did you hear that?" It was the name the Shans had given him, after he'd begun his searches for the missing.

"I told you, Loman; we researched you. We really are filmmakers, you know. Serious ones. Dead serious." She sneered. "'The One Who Carries the Dead.' You are the dead, mate. The dead and the missing." Charlene's face tightened. "Loman, our deal is still on. You still take us north."

"I'm going to Aung Khin. You and your living camera go on that ride, you may well be both missing and dead."

"We're paying you."

He sipped the beer and shrugged. "Just put the coins on your own eyes."

"We'll be met by someone before you get to Aung Khin. You can still come with us, at that point."

Loman sat up. "What the hell do you mean, you'll be met?"

"You wouldn't be harmed. Just given a choice again."

"What about you?"

"That's when we say 'ta, *Kon Ahn* et cetera."

"Like you said, you bought the ticket. Get off whenever you want."

They were far enough north now, he thought, for Taksin's contact to show up. The air was getting cooler. Loman went into the back of the van, rummaged in his AWOL bag, and took out a sweatshirt. While he had the bag open, he found and took out the transmitter Weyland had given him. He pushed the send button twice, signaling a frequency check. The red light on the oblong black shape blinked back obligingly at him. For all he knew it was a kid's toy.

He went back to his seat. Usama was filming out of the window, humming to himself like the motor of the camera.

Charlene was sitting behind him. She folded her arms across the top of his seat and rested her chin on them.

"How are you doing?" she said, her voice gentled as if it had been hushed by the country, by the same high lonely it had put into Loman's chest. He didn't know what to say to her.

He saw Win glance at them in the mirror.

"Usama said you reminded him of a priest. Did you take a vow of silence?"

Loman shrugged. He had taken a vow not to respond to bullshit.

"Not that talking isn't overrated." She nodded at the seat next to her. Usama had put down the camera and was sleeping, his face calm and blank as a screen. "I usually just point. Select. Edit. Sam and I would go weeks without speaking. But up here, I'm talky. Up here they got things that can eat you, right, Win, you bleeder."

"Heart and soul, mama."

"There's one now," she said.

Loman followed her gaze and felt a shock in his stomach. An American Armored Personnel Carrier was sticking out of the forest, its front blocking half the road. As they drew closer, he could see its treads were shattered and there were rips in the olive metal of its flanks, as if it had been clawed. There were still U.S. Army markings on it, a serial number and a stenciled line "Done Got Em." One of the gifts of Loman's youth, a detritus, like shells from ancient seas, left high and dry on this mountain. The machine was empty and torn, but the motion and power was still frozen into its blunt shape so that he could picture it as the broken point of some column that had thrust well oiled and blind with technological confidence into the enveloping jungle. Charlene shoved Usama. His eyes clicked open. He saw the APC and got his camera to the window.

"You Yanks left piles of droppings everywhere in your panicky little flight, didn't you?" Charlene asked.

Win hawked and spit out of the window as he swerved around the nose of the APC.

"You promised us some food, Win," Charlene said. There was a tension in her voice that made Loman look at her. She squeezed his hand.

"Real soon," Win said. "Jus ahead. Village I know."

"Christ, why did you have me wet the bushes then?"

"You see toilet there, you doan ask."

Charlene nodded, her eyes still locked with Loman's.

They drove a few more miles before the village appeared: a string of bamboo hootches lining both sides of the narrow road.

"Relax," Charlene said, as if to herself.

Win pulled in next to a hut with a straw awning shading the area in front of its entrance. Flimsy card tables and bamboo stools were set in the shade. A Shan woman was splashing water from a bowl onto the dust to keep it down. Turbaned Shan men sat at two of the tables, the smoke from their cheroots and beedies curling up into the thatch. They were bare-chested and heavily tattooed with animistic figures. The strand of pine and oak, northern trees, next to the hootch had been hung with temple bells in case, Loman thought, somebody forget where they were. Charlene dug her fingernails into his arm. He pulled away.

"Right," she muttered. "You sod."

Win got out of the van and stretched, then walked briskly

away. Loman and the others sat at one of the outdoor tables. It was striped with the light coming through the thatch. Charlene leaned over and whispered to the camera that stuck like an artificial proboscis from Usama's face. The Shans sitting at the other tables looked at them and shuddered. One made a demon-repelling sign with his fingers. Another stared at Loman. He whispered something to the man next to him, maybe *Kon Ahn Harm Kon Die*, though Loman wasn't sure. He didn't think he had ever been here. But stories traveled as fast as dreams in the mountains. Weapons: old M-1 carbine, Garands, an Enfield, rested against the tables where the Shans sat.

"Is this the place?" he asked Charlene.

"I don't know, man. Maybe. Relax." Her own face was twitching.

The woman who had been wetting the dust came out with bottles of Mandalay beer, a big, communal bowl of red Shan rice and sausage, a plate of pomelos and long yams, and a stack of wooden dishes. She looked at them with bold curiosity.

The men stared at them eating, whispering Loman's secret name. It caught in the wind bells, tinkled all around him. He scooped some of the rice with his fingers. It had pieces of cooked tomatoes in it, and it was spiced and cold and delicious.

Another woman came out of the hootch, carrying oblongs of rice wrapped in banana leaves in her hands. She wasn't Shan. There was something peripheral and elusive about her, Loman getting the impression she would shimmer away if he turned to look at her directly. At almost the instant the image occurred to him, she was solidly there in front of him, squat, her face dark and smooth-tough, like well-oiled teak except for the thick kohl lines outlining her eyes. In her fifties, Loman imagined, though age was always hard to tell with the hill tribespeople, and he presumed that's what she was: her hair drawn back in a tight bun, red Kachin pants under a red skirt, an armorlike mantle of silver disks on her shoulders.

"I'm Soe," she said. "You call me Auntie."

Loman looked at her again. "No, I don't think so."

Usama was filming his reaction. He saw Charlene grinning with relief. She caught his eye and nestled her head against Usama's shoulder, then kissed his neck, sucking at his skin until he winced. She caressed the small wound she had made, her eyes bright, fastened to Loman's. Loman saw the faces of the Shans at the other tables crease with disgust.

"Let's do this fast," Charlene said to the woman. "The driver will be back. Come on, Loman. What'll it be? Get off the pot."

The Shan woman came out with more beer. She looked at Loman's plate, it was empty, and called out something to the men at the other tables. They laughed loudly. One man held his nose and hawked noisily into the dust. Auntie Soe smiled.

"She said that white men have the worst, most bad-smelling farts. She said you came here because Shan food makes your belly sweet. Be careful. Shan girl starts worrying about your bowels, it means she likes you."

"That's a fascinating bit of folklore, Auntie," Charlene said, looking around. "Can we move on to the next attraction now, please mum?"

One of the men was scowling at the woman. He said something sharply to the others. Loman heard the word "*Taan*" repeated a few times in the sentence. The man smiled at him apologetically and offered the jug he was holding across the space between their tables. *Taan* meant lord, excellency. It was what the Shans called Aung Khin.

"Christ," Charlene gritted her teeth, "we're down among 'em."

Usama filmed the man.

Loman drank deeply from the jug. The wine was strong and tasted grainy and warmed his chest.

"It's good," he said. "Thank you."

The man laughed, his mouth a Technicolor flash: rubies and jade inlaid to his teeth. "Yes, yes." He picked up a Garand and aimed it at Usama, then pantomimed shooting him. He laughed more.

"What are you, Loman?" Charlene asked. "The fucking peace corps?"

"The people here," Auntie Soe said, as if explaining to her, "love Aung Khin. He helps the Shan, buys their product, marries their women, gives them money and guns to fight the Burmese."

"That's the bloody point, isn't it Auntie?" Charlene said. "As in, let's go."

Auntie Soe looked off dreamily, touching the bells dangling near the table, caressing them lightly.

"You shut up now," she said softly. "Don't worry about the driver; he has a girlfriend here. We need to wait, maybe ten minutes, someone will meet us. We need to wait. More important, after we wait, we need to go, Loman. You and me. To go to Taksin."

Loman said, "I promised these two a lift. I didn't agree to come."

"You promised Sadong also."

"You got some time to kill?" Loman said. "Tell me about Sadong."

"Tell me a story, Auntie," Charlene said. "Just take your bloody time."

Auntie smiled. "Which story do you want about Sadong? Which *pwe*?

"In theatre," Usama said without lowering the camera, "I

prefer the classical. The heroic young prince. The evil sorcerer. The beautiful princess."

Auntie Soe nodded. "A *Zat Pwe.* Something like the Warlord's Daughter? I'll give you that one. Once upon a time in Taunggyi there was a Shan *Sawbaw* who the young Khin's boss, the general of the Ninety-third, had to pay off to get his caravans through. Khin being Khin, he didn't like it, he said kill the Sawbaw, chop the head off the snake. But his boss figured the man had too many connections, army, family; it was cheaper to pay his tariff. And he thought he had better teach his young subordinate the ways of the world. So every week the general had Khin go to the *Sawbaw*'s big house and wait in the hall with the houseboy until the big shot came out and took money from him. Khin would stand, listening to the family at its meal, talking and laughter that stabbed his heart like a knife because he thought they must be laughing at him, this hungry, ragged jungle wallah waiting like a servant in the hall. And each time he came, the *Sawbaw*'s little daughter—spoiled, treated like a princess—would peek at him while he was in the hallway, as if he were a *deva* from the forest, a spirit brought by her father to scare her into good behavior. Khin saw this child every time he came to the house. He saw her get beautiful. Then one day he shot her father, shot the Ninety-third general, went into business on his own, and took the girl. Traditional drama. Boy meets girl."

"That was Sadong?" Loman asked.

Auntie Soe whacked Loman's knee. "Maybe. Some think that. But one other classical version is, that was only the roots of fate. That Sadong was the daughter of Khin and that *Sawbaw*'s child. That his wife died when she was young. Some say she was killed by the Burmese. Others say Khin spent each day of their marriage making her pay for the time he spent waiting in her father's hall until either he killed her or she killed herself. Whichever is true, if either, she left him a daughter, a beautiful girl he saw as coming from him like a lotus from the mud."

"Like a rose from a turd," Charlene muttered.

"Sure. He thought he was shit, but when he looked at her, he thought maybe not. He played the *Sawbaw*, gave her whatever she wanted; when she got older, he sent her to university in Rangoon. She grew up, she went her own way. Then one day he looks at her and she is dead in his heart. Why? Who knows? Maybe he didn't like that she got involved in the freedom riots. Maybe she asked about her mother. Maybe one day she told him she didn't like where the money that paid for her clothing and schools came from, that he was shit after all. Okay, he thinks, if he is shit, he better act his nature. Or maybe he just looked at her one day and saw a face and body, eyes that looked away from his eyes; he saw this woman who wasn't a part of him. Not a part of Taan to Taan means dead. And Taan likes to use the dead."

"I've heard the daughter story too," Charlene shrugged. "It could be true; it doesn't have to be an opera. Who else but family could the big one trust working for him in Bangkok? But it isn't the only version of the legend, is it, Auntie?"

Auntie Soe looked out the door, her face suddenly tired. "The other is the *Nat Pwe*, the forbidden *pwe*. The *pwe* of darkness and forbidden desires. We won't speak of the other."

Loman remembered Sadong talking about what she did for Khin, when he came to Bangkok. He felt his throat thicken.

"Once upon a time," he said, "there was a little girl who lived in a palace of white poppies in a country far to the north."

"Good on you," Charlene said. "Exit stage left, end of play. Which is true? You put up your soul, you puts your arse on the line, you takes your choice. What's it going to be

Loman? Come with us. Ask Taksin for the truth. Taksin is an even better story."

Auntie Soe squinted at Loman. "In theatre," she said, spitting a stream of betel nut, "like Usama, I prefer the traditional."

Loman turned. A line of men in olive fatigues were pointing weapons at the table. In the center of the line, holding an AK-47 casually in one hand, was the man who had killed the German in his bar. The man touched the wedge of scar tissue on his neck and smiled at Loman.

"Us," he whispered hoarsely.

"Shit," Charlene said.

"He's the fucking Hobbit," Fat Al groaned, squinting after Weyland. "And we're the fat little fucking dwarves."

They panted behind Weyland's squat form, darting ahead on the nearly invisible path through the jungle.

Harry tried to consider Weyland as a hobbit. But whatever comic possibilities the red-headed man might have provided had been left back in Bangkok. He was at ease, as competent in the jungle as he had been with every other aspect of their trip. They'd driven up through the flat paddy land around Chiang Mai, taken a raft two days up the Mekong, all without any guide except Weyland. A jeep had been waiting for them at the village where they'd landed. Weyland had the keys. He'd driven them for about a mile along the wide path that ambled north out of the village, then abruptly turned into what seemed a solid wall of jungle. Instead they'd slipped onto a bumpy little mud ribbon.

Weyland stopped walking. He turned and smiled at Harry, as if he'd read his mind. A broken beam of light fell on his face. His redness, Harry noted, had spread down into his skin some natural colorization emerging the farther they went into the jungle. Weyland didn't seem discomfited by the sunburn. He didn't seem to sweat either. Maybe Fat Al saw hobbit, but Harry experienced something cool and snaky emerging here.

"You okay?" Weyland asked him. Mama serpent.

"No problem."

Fat Al slapped Mundy on the back. "We humping it, right senator?"

Mundy, staring at the jungle, nodded absently, affirming an answer to a question only he was hearing.

"Green hell," Chuckie said.

Actually, the jungle wasn't as bad as Harry had imagined it would be when Weyland had stopped the jeep and said they'd have to go on foot the rest of the way. He liked being here, insects, clinging vines, weird birds, and all. He felt a sense of military comfort; he'd put one foot in front of the other, get where he was going. Everything narrowed to a path.

Which ended, with his comfort, in a field of bamboo, the stalks towering five or six feet over their heads. A few yards into it and Harry felt swallowed. The plants wrapped around and over him; the air sat heavy as mold in his lungs. Weyland flowed through the thick poles. Harry tried to stay close behind him, the stalks whipping back into his face.

They stopped and emerged onto a clearing, checkered with corn and bean patches. A village of about thirty bamboo-sided thatched-roof houses was spread on top of the low hill in front of them.

A mob of yapping dogs and giggling children poured from it, more kids joining in as they got closer, imitating the nervous jerkiness of the men's walk. Fat Al scowled at them and wiped his face. "Di-di the hell outta here," he said. The children mimicked his croak delightedly.

"Manners, Mr. Reisling," Weyland said. His red flesh, Harry noted, was as dry as when they'd started.

"What the hell are you, Weyland—the goddam chamber of commerce?"

"No, man," Chuckie giggled. "He's the mayor."

Harry wished they would both shut up.

Some kids ran up next to him, wide-eyed, pointing at his skin. One little boy, naked except for a black shirt, reached out to touch Harry's cheek, then drew his hand back as if it had been burned. Harry grinned at him and the boy laughed in delight. He'd been up country in Thailand before and was used to the reaction to his skin color.

In the village now. Fat black pigs nuzzled Harry's legs like the victims of an enchantment. Between the houses he saw women, their dresses embroidered with bright splashes of color. They were grinding rice between stone wheels, feeding the pigs, walking out to the gardens with hoes over their shoulders, washing their long black hair and tossing it to dry. Turbaned, black-clad men with ancient rifles or crossbows slung on their shoulders lolled around, watching. The men's clothing, so like VC pajamas, made Harry nervous. One man began blowing into what looked like a bunch of bamboo pipes tied together with twine. This strange, wavering music to mark their entering parade.

"*Kaen* flute," Weyland explained to Mundy. "They're welcoming us."

Mundy smiled at him and nodded, his eyes bright. Harry saw Al glance at Chuckie and snort.

Weyland was *wai*-ing to the people. They surrounded him, spoke excitedly to him, some of them reaching out and rubbing and patting the redness of his skin. He answered them in their own language, whatever he said raising a ripple of laughter. Al burped, reached over and patted one of the pigs possessively. He waved around. "I wish I had a village," he said, "to plunder and pillage."

They stopped in front of a large house, its thatched roof

overhanging the sides and creating a cool shaded area. A middle-aged woman with a square, competent-looking face came out and *wai*-ed to Weyland. She wore more strands of the silver coins than he'd seen on the other women.

"Surit is the headman's wife," Weyland explained to Mundy. "Gentlemen, we'll come inside for a while."

Mundy did an exaggerated *wai*, dipping his head too low. The headman's wife gave him a puzzled look. As Harry filed past her, she stared at him, then touched her own cheek as if to check its color. She said something laughingly to Weyland.

"They think you're some kind of demon," Weyland explained. "They reacted the same way to my red hair and complexion when I first came."

"What made them change their mind?"

"Not a thing," Weyland said.

They stepped into the cool darkness of the house. Two old women were cooking, stirring an iron cauldron hung over an indoor fire, the kids playing behind them. The smoke hung in the air. Harry saw a gaunt man squatting in front of a spirit shelf in one corner: an arrangement of bones, small antlers, squiggles of dried intestines on it. The woman, Surit, disappeared behind a partition. Fat Al walked to the shelf and began to finger some of the objects, as if considering whether they were edible. The gaunt man slapped his hand.

"Touchy fucker, isn't he?" Fat Al said.

"Where's the headman?" Mundy asked.

"Indisposed."

Weyland pointed to the shadows at the far side of the house. As Harry's watering eyes adjusted more he saw an old man lying stark naked on a bamboo sleeping platform raised about a foot off the floor, his body striped with shadow, his eyes half-slit open. He cradled a long pipe against his scrawny chest.

"Opium?" Mundy asked.

Fat Al snickered.

Weyland looked at the congressman with a lazy, open contempt that startled Harry.

The woman came out, her long hair wrapped up into a beehive. "Surit's the real headman," Weyland said, smiling at her. Surit nodded, as if she'd understood. She sat with them while the old women fed them on leaf plates. Dinner, as far as Harry could tell, was fat frogs, wild boar, and a haunch of local dog. Surit and Weyland chattered through it, two people catching up on news and gossip.

Fat Al ate noisily, licking his fingers. The people from the hut whispered to each other and giggled at Al's appetite. One of the house chickens had stopped its pecking and was looking at Fat Al, as if in astonishment. The old woman offered him a bowl of dried cicadas. Al picked up one and sucked it noisily, grinning at Mundy. The little legs hung crookedly out of his mouth. Mundy grimaced.

"Hey, senator," Al said, snapping his fingers as if he'd just remembered something. He snatched up the chicken, stuffed its head into his mouth, tore it off with his teeth, and spit it on the floor. The body jerked a little then flopped, a puddle of blood pulsing out of the neck and soaking into the swept dirt. Feathers hung on the corners of Fat Al's mouth. The old woman screamed at him shrilly. The kids started crying.

"For Christ's sake, Al," Chuckie said, "that was probably fucking Rover."

Surit stood and began complaining in a high-pitched voice, her face creased with anger. Weyland sighed deeply.

"Reisling," he said. "Go outside."

Fat Al picked his teeth, looking at Weyland through narrowed eyes, then nodded. He rose lazily and went out. Chuckie and Harry and the others came after him. Weyland came last. He spoke to one of the male villagers. The man grimaced and called out a long, shrill command. A silent line of male villagers gathered behind Weyland. Something heavy rolled over in Harry's stomach.

"What's up, Red?" Fat Al picked his teeth.

"You'll mind your manners," Weyland said softly. "In my home."

They were looking at each other across a yard of yellow dirt. "Your home? You talking that stinking hootch, Red? Or, like the whole scene?" He reached over and grabbed a little boy. The child started crying. Fat Al rumpled his hair, let him go. The boy ran to his mother. "The famous exploding shoeshine boy," he said to Chuckie, then turned to Mundy. "See, you gotta be careful, senator, not to go Asiastic. Remember, the whole country's against you. Even the babies are cocked and loaded." He burped loudly. "Geez, I'm being impolite again. So whatcha going to do, Red, make me a lance corporal and send me to the Golden Triangle?"

Weyland smiled at him disarmingly. "Maybe I'll just make you a cook. Like what you were."

Al's eyes were locked to Weyland's.

"Knock it off," Chuckie said.

"Says Chuckie's-in-Love." Weyland considered him. "How's your love life, Chuckie? Whore-wise? Chuckie's war, congressman, he kept hatting out to Saigon, hiding out with the whores, till the navy gave him six-six and a kick. That's six months in the brig, six months forfeiture of pay, and a bad paper discharge, Mr. Mundy. For your ever-expanding military vocabulary."

"You mess with the bull," Fat Al said, grinning, shrugging, "you get the shit." He stepped forward, his hands curling.

Weyland said something softly. One of the villagers, a wide young man with *naga* tattoos coiled around his arms, moved, Harry having a hard time following it: a step to the side, a blurred motion of hands and feet and Fat Al was sitting on the ground clutching his groin, his legs splayed out. The villagers tittered appreciatively.

Fat Al lay his head back down in the dust. A pig nudged him. "My methods were unsound," Fat Al said to it.

Harry grabbed Chuckie's arm and held him.

Weyland looked down. "Let's just keep our mouth off the operation from now on, Reisling. You think you can do that? You think you can shut your mouth?"

Fat Al sat up and winked at him. "Tell you what. You feel froggy," he said. "Wart."

Weyland made a plucking gesture, as if he were releasing a bow string. The young man's foot whipped out. Fat Al's head snapped back in the dust. Chuckie and Harry both stepped forward. Hands grabbed them, held them fast. The young man did a lazy shuffle-and-jab pantomime, kick-boxed the air.

"Mr. Weyland, I want this stopped," Mundy said.

"Do you, congressman?" Weyland said pleasantly. "Want to put a rein on things, do you? Lay out some rules of engagement?"

Al picked his head up. "Sounds good to me, you red-headed little prick."

This time Harry didn't even see Weyland gesture, only the *naga*-tattooed man kicking out again.

"Weyland, enough," Harry said. "He gets the point. We all do."

"Is that true, Mr. Reisling?"

Fat Al muttered something. He spat out a tooth.

"I can't hear you."

"Enough," Harry said. "Or I don't fly for you, man."

Weyland gave him a mock bow. He gestured and the *naga*-tattooed man stepped back into the crowd. "Helicopter Harry," Weyland said. Harry stood and waited, snake-stare fixed himself now. "The last member of our little Medal of Honor society." He assessed Harry gravely.

Mundy frowned at Weyland. "Do we really need to establish a schoolyard pecking order here, Art?"

"No violence in the war zone, huh congressperson?" Weyland said.

The scar-necked man glided up to Charlene, seized her throat, and brought her up and out of the seat. Loman swung at the scar. He missed, fanning air. The other men swarmed him, shouting. Someone rifle-butted him in the kidney. Nausea swam up into his mouth. He leaned forward, trying to vomit, but his arms were grabbed, locked tight, and he swallowed a thin, bitter stream of bile.

Charlene was standing, rubbing her neck. "What were you going to do, Yank, rescue me?"

One of the men slapped her.

"Thanks anyway," she said. The man slapped her again.

Auntie Soe, Loman saw, was gone. He saw Charlene notice it too.

"Bloody bitch," she said.

They were hustled to the van, Usama clutching his camera to his breast. Win was standing in front of the vehicle, shirtless and shivering, his *longyi* drooping. There were two jeeps, one in front and one behind the van. One of the men motioned them inside, then got in after them. He sat in the back seat and kept his weapon pointed at them.

They drove out of the village. The road wound downhill into a forest of teak and palms and narrowed to a packed mud path, the branches of the trees arched thickly over it. Oval leaves and branches scraped the windows and the sides of the van. Where there were gaps in the overhead foliage, bamboo latticework had been erected; it formed a close roof over the trail.

Loman lost all sense of time in the semidarkness of the tunnel; when they emerged into the burning daylight on the crest of a ridge, he was no longer even sure of the day. The trees had been cleared in ragged patches, slash-and-burn fields that seemed torn from the hillside as if someone had pulled off scabs. Potatoes and tobacco were growing in some of them, but mostly they were thick with poppies, carpet squares of gleaming white. Shan women, tin cans hung around their necks, were bending over and nicking the poppy pods. The narrow road started to wind down the steep hill. Loman could see to the valley below. Rows of long concrete buildings were losing their shapes into lengthening shadows. Several lights blinked on as he watched, feeble sparks against the dark mountains.

"Velcome to Castle Dracula," Charlene said.

A guard turned and yelled in Shan at her.

From the pattern of lights, it seemed the camp was laid out in a rough *T* shape. He imagined it would be hard to spot unless an aircraft flew straight over it. Loman made out two humped shapes at the base. He was sure they were helicopters.

The inner perimeter of the camp was marked by a line of sandbag bunkers spaced among the trees. A guard waved them through an open barbed-wire gate. They drove past several clusters of low, concrete buildings that had the joyless, functional look of the elementary schools Loman remembered dimly from the run-down areas of Billings, where he had grown up. One of them had an open blacktop area like a playground and a flagpole in front of it. There was no flag and the playground was stacked with bundles of opium.

They drove past an open field. The sun was completely gone now, but it was a full moon and Loman could make out several log obstacles and an open pit with a log thrown across it. A line of men were low-crawling through the tangle of bushes in the field. The crawlers were stabbing the earth in front of them, with long knives or bayonets. The line would stop, stab, rise to its collective knees as if to pray: each man extending his arms above his head, then bringing them down very slowly as if the air had thickened, until they would gently pat the earth they'd wounded. There must have been a hundred of them in the field. Loman wondered why an opium army was training in mine and booby-trap clearing.

"Lost their contacts, have they?" Charlene said. Loman put a hand on her shoulder and felt her flesh tremble into his palm.

Usama looked at them and turned away. He brought his camera up, pointing it out of the window. The guard behind him screamed. The jeep in front of the van stopped and their driver cursed and braked. The white man with the scarred neck flew back to them and pushed the camera hard into Usama's eye. He screamed and lowered it, a red crescent marring his comic-book smooth face. The scar-necked man smiled and jabbed the barrel of his weapon through the open window and into Usama's eye. The jab was almost casual, but there was a brutal push at the end of the motion and Loman heard a sickening, grape-squishing noise. Charlene and Usama both screamed. Usama clutched his face, blood welling darkly between his fingers.

The man pointed the AK-47 at Loman. The end of the barrel was wet.

"You come with me," he grunted. It was his longest sentence. In spite of the tiger-striped army fatigues and the GI jungle boots and the bracelets, he wasn't American; Loman couldn't place the accent.

"What about these people?" Loman said. "He needs help."

"Now."

Loman squeezed Charlene's shoulder again.

The man walked behind him and prodded him with the barrel. They walked to a building on the other side of the field. There was a blacktop like the other one Loman had seen, burlap bundles stacked on it. Loman could see the number 4 and a print of a coiled serpent on each, a silent, incantatory pattern of numbers and snakes. A ten-foot-high wall of bundles formed a barrier in the middle of the blacktop. They walked to the other side. A volleyball net had been set up there. A heavy brown-skinned man in his sixties wearing tailored olive fatigues was sitting in a leather chair under a kerosene lantern hung from one net pole. The man's face was bland with power. Loman recognized him from pictures he'd seen. He sat about six feet from the wall of opium, looking at a blank big-screen television set. He had a remote in his hands. An orange cable ran from behind the set to a loudly chugging portable generator. Aung Khin looked up at Loman. He seemed bored.

"Mundy sent me," Loman said, feeling absurd.

Khin sighed.

"Now you offer me expensive scotch and reveal your fiendish plan to me in its entirety because you've been waiting for someone of intelligence who could appreciate its evil genius," Loman tried.

Khin waved at the scar-necked man. He came forward and put a tape into a VCR. Loman wondered if it was the one he had taken from Usama.

"Later," he continued, "I escape by the skin of my teeth. Look, I am from Mundy." He shifted uneasily.

Khin said, "I understand you appreciate *pwes* and classical dramas. There's one Burmese tale in which a king tries to kill a popular young rebel who flees to the forest, and so the king marries his sister. After they shared their bed, the king tells her that her brother was now his brother and could return from the jungle. When he does, the king has him tied to a *saga* tree and burned to death. When the girl sees her brother's flesh curling in the flames, she breaks away from the king and embraces the boy and their flesh melts together. Their souls fly into the tree and the two of them become nats of the *saga* tree. Do you like my story?"

"I prefer happy endings," Loman said.

"That was a happy ending," Khin said.

Loman sensed the movement to his right, too late. The butt of the rifle was as big as the side of a ship.

Now he was in the chair. He thought it was nice of Khin to stand. Khin and his man seemed to want him to watch television with them. He watched a show run backward in which he seemed to be the star. Loman in the Shan village, Loman in the van, Loman sitting on a bench under the Shwedagon, receiving the wisdom that would lead to freedom from the suffering of existence. No sound. His own face, staring at Sadong's anxious face, was ugly with hunger. Khin seemed to like that part. He paused it. He rewound it. He fast-forwarded it. He paused it again.

"Why make a myth out of a murder?" Loman asked him.

For the first time, Khin smiled.

Two of Khin's men reached down from a great distance and hauled Loman to his feet. One of them was the scar-necked man. They crowded in on Loman, screaming, grabbing his arms from behind. The man in front of him drew his knee back in slow motion, in moonlight. The searing pain shooting up from his crotch brought him back to clarity. The man smiled at him. Us, he said. Loman went limp, sagging, letting the man holding him from behind take the weight, then twisted suddenly free and continued the motion around, slamming his fist into the rise of scar tissue on his neck. The man screamed and grabbed at his neck as if he were choking himself. "Me," Loman said. Khin said something sharply, and more guards fell on him. The other man grabbed his arms again. Someone hit Loman in the face with a rifle butt.

When he opened his eyes again, he saw a stone in front of them. Its pitted and mottled surface seemed wonderfully intricate, as if it contained the geography of a complete planet with its own laws and customs. Loman stared at it, lonely as a misunderstood deity. He looked up into whorls of stars dusted on an ink-black sky. Khin's moon face replaced the heavens. Loman moved his head. Everyone was still here except the scar-necked man. Now he was truly missing, Loman thought, and giggled. Khin said something sharply. A Shan girl, her face twisted with disgust, emptied a jar of cold water on him.

The guards took Loman's arms and pulled him to his feet. Maybe there was a custom against being shot while you were down. His face felt on fire and he still tasted vomit in his mouth. One of the guards tied his hands behind him. Loman thought he would die now. He found he felt detached from the fact of it; it was just another part of the dream. His vision was suddenly cut off. In the blackness, he felt a coarse, heavy binding nestling into the hollows of his eyes. A surge of panic burst his groggy complacency. The thought came to him that he had been shot, he was dead, that this was death, an eternal feeling of heavy cloth pressing and closing his senses, trapping his awareness beneath it. Hands were clutching him, lifting him. He was thrown, landing hard and rolling over, his back pushing against a more yielding hardness. He heard the slide of a door, through the cloth, and was aware that the coolness of air on the rest of his skin was cut off. Someone turned an ignition key. The floor vibrated beneath him.

He lay still as a bundle, bouncing as the vehicle hit rough places, trying to listen. If people were in with him besides the driver, they said nothing. Loman sat up and began inching backward on his butt, his tied hands waving behind him like exploring antennae.

The driver down-shifted.

Loman had to rest, his head throbbing. He stretched out his legs. It felt suddenly luxurious. He regarded the feeling with vast amusement. The small pleasures of the flesh, now and at the moment of death.

He donned all the gear that as a REMF he never wore: helmet, flak jacket, bandoliers of ammo, web belt hung with canteens and magazines, his M-16. He put it all on like a kid dressing up. Jambeau, a French photographer who liked to play on the edge, had dared him to hitchhike into Hue. He and Jambeau marched out of the base camp between an honor guard of piss tubes and MPs who waved them out on Jambeau's press pass and looked at them as if they were already dead. The MPs waved Loman down the hotel hallway, out through the barbed wire behind which he'd huddled for months, growing stale and fat. Something opened in him. He was going to Hue. After months behind the wire he was determined to see if anything really existed out there. He and Jambeau walked out into it, where Americans didn't go except in patrol or convoy. They took it by surprise. It was as if they had walked into a theatre before the players were ready to slip into the roles they only assumed when being watched. Women stood motionless in the paddies. Pedicab drivers were stopped in their tracks. The palm trees neglected to rustle. The strong sun poured a curious blankness over everything. Then, as if noticing the two foreigners, the scene came belatedly to life. A jitney bus top-heavy with people and baskets and pigs stopped, and Loman and Jambeau hung from the back, the heaviness of their equipment nearly pulling them off as they bounced down the Street Without Joy, singing "Follow the Yellow Brick Road." When Loman grinned at the passengers, the whole bus laughed crazily, bouncing past the mile markers to Hue. Follow, follow, follow, follow, follow the yellow brick road. *He chased Kitty down the corridor into Hue with Jambeau and his fake press pass, two spacemen in their equipment, walking on a planet of lesser gravity. Sadong danced just ahead. He passed piles of rubble waiting to spring into configurations of temples and palaces as he rounded corners. He and Jambeau ran through the mossy coolness of time, past split mimosa trees, ran down the hallways of the Hotel Miami, Bangkok, ran along the banks of the River of Perfumes, past the shattered citadel and ancient palaces cracked like eggs. Behind the façade of each street was a blankness. The river was red and clogged with mud and corpses, bits and pieces.*

That's disgusting, Usama said.

He woke to a trickle of cold air and the realization of where he was. It was like waking from a drunk. Everything that had seemed so amusing the night before was no longer funny. The cloth was smothering him, blinding him; when he began to hyperventilate, he sucked the cloth into his nostrils and felt himself suffocating. He tried to control his breathing, slow it down. He had no idea how long he had been out.

He sat very still.

Something was in here with him. He could hear nothing but the sound of the motor, whining in low gear. But he sensed a presence. The hair on his wrists and on the back of his neck was standing up. He edged himself up and began scuttling backward. His hands touched the metal frame, then the vinyl upholstery of a seat. There was nothing on it. He worked his way backward to the next seat. His hand, groping behind, brushed something on the floor and he held back a cry. Some kind of rough cloth. A blanket. He moved his hands over it tentatively. There was a hard shape under it. He could feel himself start to hyperventilate again with the need to move away. But his tied hands still patted as if they had a will of their own. They found the edge of the blanket, hesitated, then went under and up. Soft ice. A face. Nose, closed eyes, the skin dry and cold. The mouth was open. His blind fingers explored the contours of the face. He was aware of the cloth touching his own face. He had the notion that this was his own corpse, left behind.

The vehicle swerved sharply and the body rolled against his back. He braced his legs against the opposite seat and muscled the weight back up with his shoulders. His hands kept searching, fingering. Boney shoulders. Breasts, their icy heaviness rolling in his hands.

What have you done to us, Yank?

He thought how she had been in the village when Khin's men took them. He had started to like her.

"The modern dilemma, mate," he said.

His hands found her fingers, rigid, curved into claws. He got his face down next to them, moving it back and forth until he could feel a rigid finger, two, slip under the edge of his blindfold. A scream started to well in his throat. He bit his lips to keep it in, then gave up and let it burst as he pulled his face back and down, the corpse's nails raking his skin, but the blindfold lifting. His vision focused slowly, sunlight burning in his eyes. Sadong's face, a puzzled smile on her lips, assembled in front of him.

dead weight grew and shifted in Harry's stomach. But he followed Weyland anyway, just like Mundy and Chuckie and Al did, came after him because he had no place else to go.

They went out of the village, down into another cleared valley, then through more bamboo. The plants scraped open something in his mind and let in pictures, names. He followed Weyland just like the rest of them, looking at last for a victory.

They came out of the bamboo and climbed to the crest of another hill. Harry stopped and looked below.

It was a standard landing zone, about two hundred feet in diameter, hacked and burned raggedly out of the jungle. A thatched-roof bamboo hut next to the jungle on one side. The helicopter in the middle.

He walked to it, watching his shadow grow smaller on it as he got closer, until he reached out and touched the cold curve of its metal skin.

Loman's cheeks burned with Sadong's scratches. He was in the same vehicle with the same passengers. Charlene's wide-eyed frozen stare was mirrored by the open *O* of her mouth. Her chin and throat bulged. Something that looked like the bald head of a baby bird peeked out of her mouth. Blood had dried black and crusted on her chin. Loman glanced at the stain at Usama's crotch, then looked away. He wondered why they always came back to this one. He had never understood the message. He felt like vomiting, but there was nothing left. He inched toward Charlene; he couldn't leave her clogged. The sunlight pouring in the van's windows was painful after the blindfold. Win looked at him over his shoulder. He was wearing olive fatigues. His face was stiff with fear.

The windshield shattered inward. Win fought the wheel and braked hard, the van swerving close to the side of the narrow road. The bodies rolled, landing around Loman, their cold flesh smothering. Loman whimpered, trying to free himself. He saw Win was shaking violently, his small shoulders hunching under his fatigues. He turned to Loman again. His eyes were closed and his cheeks were wet with tears. He seemed as much a prisoner as Loman. As if to prove it, he slowly raised his hands, lacing his fingers behind his neck.

A shadow passed the window near Loman. The barrel of an AK-47 came through the driver's side and pressed against Win's head. The noise of the shot was tremendous in the closed space. A thick rope of blood flew across the front seat and pulled Win after it, slamming him against the opposite window. Loman shook.

Auntie Soe poked her head into the driver's door. She looked around, then disappeared.

The side door slid open. Auntie Soe asked Loman something, but his ears were still ringing. He shook his head. She climbed inside. When she saw the bodies she stopped. When she saw Sadong, her face brittled with grief. She put the weapon down and touched Sadong's face, sucking in a sharp gasp of air.

She muttered to herself and shook her head, then rewrapped the blanket around Sadong and pulled her out of the tangle of bodies and through the door. When she came back, she had a kukri knife in her hand. She got behind Loman. The flesh on his neck crawled in anticipation. When the bonds on his wrists came apart, the tension in his stomach snapped with them. He rubbed his wrists, then went to Charlene and pulled the fleshy mass from her mouth and closed it, then her eyes.

Outside, Auntie Soe was squatting next to Sadong's body, her eyes closed, her lips moving. She seemed an old, grieving woman. Loman found it hard to connect her to what he had just seen her do to Win. She dragged Sadong's body back a little farther, into the trees on the side of the road. Loman started to go back inside to get the others.

"Come here," she yelled to him.

"They need to be buried too."

"Come here, *Kon Ahn Harm Kon Die.*" She pointed the AK-47 at him. He walked over to her. She braced her feet wide and fired a long burst into the van. The gas tank went, the heat slapping Loman's face. He stood and watched it burn.

"You set us up," he said to her.

"And that's why I'm here," she said with disgust.

Loman closed his eyes. It was true—if she was Khin's plant, why would she ambush the van?

"Why did you shoot that boy?" he asked her.

She waved the barrel of her weapon at Sadong's blanket-wrapped body.

"You take her. You carry her, *Kon Ahn Harm Kon Die,* or I'll kill you too."

Loman looked at her. "Bad movies," he said.

He squatted down and touched Sadong, brushing the hair back from her face. He pulled her up and onto his shoulders in a fireman's carry, Auntie Soe pushing from behind, helping to break her rigidity. The weight buckled his knees.

They climbed a rock-scattered, grassy slope splashed with sun. The trees thinned as they got higher. Sadong's weight pulled him backward. At the top of the ridge, Auntie Soe stopped and looked around intently. As far as Loman could see, there was nothing but other ridge lines. A pocket of gray cloud hung from the trees in the valley below, as if the ridge line bordered another climate.

"I'm going to put her down and rest," he said.

"No. Wait."

She was standing very still, listening. After a minute she said, "The boy was necessary; I didn't want us followed."

"Khin knew he would be ambushed. Hell, the kid knew it; he was waiting for it."

She nodded. "I'm afraid that is why Khin gave her to us." She put a hand on Sadong's body. "As a weight, to slow us down so he can keep up with us. So we can lead him to Taksin."

Taan likes to use the dead, Loman remembered her saying.

"I got out of it too easily, when they took you," Auntie Soe said, as though to herself. "And why else would he let you go?"

"Then we need to leave her," Loman said.

A wind was blowing strongly over the ridge. Auntie Soe closed her eyes, swaying a little, as if listening to it tell her secrets.

"I won't leave her for the jungle. Let's go."

She tossed her head and began to run down the slope on the other side of the ridge, her bag jingling against her side as she wove through the trees. He ran toward her, Sadong's hard bones and stiffening flesh bouncing against his shoulders. He felt a cold, cheesy oozing from her, coming through the blanket, mixing with his sweat. He could never be sure if he had been intimate with her, but they were flowing into each other now.

He was at the bottom, in the valley now, the ground soft with bracken that held his feet and ankles. Auntie Soe looked at him and stopped and put her hand on his arm. At her touch, he felt his body again, his heart thudding in his chest, his nerves and muscles frantically protesting. Fifteen years of Bangkok whiskey were pouring out of his skin. He felt a kind of fever lap heavily in his head.

"Move," Auntie Soe said.

"I can't carry her."

"We'll rest soon."

"You take her for a while."

"No. I can't touch her. But I will not leave her."

"We don't abandon our dead, right?" Loman said. "There are no missing."

"We don't abandon this dead. Let's go now."

The water in the stream ran clear and fast over white sand and pebbles. They splashed along in it, the current threatening to tip Loman. They climbed out and started up the opposite slope of the valley. Auntie Soe stopped every few yards, stood still, and listened, Loman coming up, panting, next to her. He could hear nothing.

When they were nearly at the top, she pointed the AK-47 at a semicircle of black jagged rocks. They picked their way into their center. Auntie Soe stopped and squatted. Loman put Sadong down, tearing her from his skin. He sat next to her. The rocks formed a protective, crenellated wall around them.

Auntie Soe unslung the large Shan shoulder bag she carried and pulled out a tight cloth cylinder, bound with twine. She unrolled a thin blanket.

"Help me."

The two of them wrapped it around the blanket already covering Sadong's body.

When they were finished, she drew out a plastic baggie full of dried prawns and two bottles of Mandalay beer, as if they had come on a picnic. Loman took one of the beers and drained it. Auntie Soe reached into the bag again and took out a small, gilded Buddha, standing, one palm upraised, and placed it in a niche in the rock. Buddha watched the three of them, his smile wistful, as if remembering Sadong playing the seer at the Shwedagon. The *Abhaya Mudra* is a posture that evokes protection and tranquillity, but it also means danger. Who tells you when it is one, when it is the other? It all depends, Sadong's voice in his mind said, as if she'd leaked into him through his skin. His head was spinning. Auntie Soe drew out another packet from her magic bag, this one marked with the snake symbol he'd seen on the bundles in Khin's camp. She removed a beautifully carved opium pipe. She put it down carefully, then turned, shifting on her knees, and prayed to the statue, touching her hands from her forehead to the ground.

When she was finished, she looked up at Loman. The peacefulness that had shelled her face cracked and fell off.

"Sleep," she said. "We'll move when it's dark. We don't need to make it easy for him."

"If you know Khin is following, why go to Taksin?"

She touched Sadong's draped form gently. "We'll lose him. Taksin will never forgive me—or you, Loman, if we leave her. I would not forgive myself. Khin knows that. But I don't think he can follow me."

It occurred to Loman again that Auntie Soe was Khin's plant, the ambush and rescue a charade. For a second he was taken by the idea. But it made no sense, Sadong's voice told him. If she knew where to go, she would simply tell Khin. Why the drama? It would be like Tom Sawyer imprisoning Jim so he could help him escape.

So how come a nice Burmese ghost like you is using American literary analogies?

I am you and you are me.

Koo koo ka choo.

Mock, Loman. But we're the brother and sister melted together, spirits seared into the heart of a tree.

You're just something I ate.

Still some wishful thinking there, eh, Loman? But you are my brother. Now and until the hour of your death.

"Sleep," Auntie Soe said.

Loman lay down next to Sadong like an obedient son.

When he awoke the sun was almost gone and Auntie Soe was at her prayers again. Loman's fever anchored him to the rock.

The resinous smell of opium hung in the air. It mixed with the smell coming from Sadong.

He felt something like the brushing of a fine feather in his mind, a stirring. Her presence.

Auntie Soe froze into her squat.

As he watched, a captive audience, she began to unwrap herself, like a mime of the slow awakening of a flower. He tried to pick his head up, but the world spun. She lifted the AK without making a sound, waved at Loman with her free hand to stay down, as if he had a choice. He could hear nothing. Wind. Then a faint clicking.

Auntie Soe lay the rifle next to Loman and disappeared over the rocks. She was gone. He couldn't remember seeing her move.

He strained to hear in the gathering darkness. The faint clicking again. He touched the AK-47. You don't do weapons, brother, Sadong's voice admonished him. Weapons are for simple tools. A real hand gripped the top of the rock across from him, then another. A face appeared, its side oozing a blackness that seemed to be dissolving into the gathering darkness of the evening. He had the thought that Charlene and Usama had come crawling after him, the abandoned dead, the missing. Auntie Soe loomed up behind the face, a possessing demon. She stroked the boy's hair gently, then quickly cut his throat. He passed into death between blinks.

She vaulted over the rock and picked up the rifle. There were more trackers behind him, she said, she hadn't wanted to shoot. She had led the rest of them off in the wrong direction, she hoped, except for this one. Could Loman move now?

"Yes."

Auntie Soe looked at him doubtfully.

■ ■ ■

Sadong's weight held him to earth. Every few minutes, Auntie Soe looked back at him to check, the shifts of the moonlight stretching and compacting her form, making her fluid. Shape Changer.

He'd lost the handle of time. It started to become light. They were high on another ridge. Below were teak trees and oak and chestnut and bamboo and pine. A strange mixture of northern and southern foliage, as if Mount Meru had shifted out of the way and Jambudipa had slid into the northern continent. There was high pine country, but it had jungle gathered in the moist pits of its valleys, all of it mantled with mist and silence and a sense of movement flickering under the mantle, things too elusive to see, busy in patterns that had nothing to do with him.

The weight on his shoulders clawed down into him.

I'm with you here, Loman. In this place.

When it became too light to risk going any farther they stopped and made camp in a small cave, high on the spine of a mountain. They put Sadong under a rock overhang. Auntie Soe helped Loman lie down, fed him, then stood up outside, parted her Kachin trousers and urinated, glancing back in at Loman with amusement, making sure he saw. Auntie was no lady. He came back inside and removed the Buddha from the bag and set it up on a small ledge, his movements as delicate and fastidious as, Loman saw now, a man dancing a woman, as his movements with the knife had been. Soon Loman heard the murmur of prayer. He lay and watched him continue the ceremony that had been interrupted by the arrival of soldiers.

 gust of wind carried Sadong's smell into the cave. It whirled around the inside of the enclosed area searching for Loman. Auntie Soe brushed his hand over his own face to sweep it away.

"I killed her by coming," Loman said.

Auntie Soe nodded. He picked up the knife he had just used. Loman sat still. Auntie Soe kneaded a ball of opium, stuck it on the point of the kukri, and heated it with the flame of a cigarette lighter. He took the softened substance outside. Loman saw him smearing it on Sadong's blanket. He came back into the cave.

"Why are you taking me to Taksin?"

Auntie Soe peered at Loman as if he were thinking it over. "Sadong made me promise to take you there. We'll rest here for a few hours, then go on. We're nearly at the camp. Tell me what you understand."

"I don't understand you."

Auntie Soe wiped the blade and held it up. "You mean what kind of Buddhist kills and then prays? A bad Buddhist, Loman."

"That's not what I meant."

Auntie Soe laughed harshly. "Oh, some people think I'm a nat, or at least a man who let a female nat into him. Who knows, maybe it's true." He held up his hand. "Listen, Loman, in the *yokthe pwe,* the puppet *pwe,* female roles are taken by male actors. I was one of the best in the country. I've done male and female roles in the *yein pwe,* the dance *pwe,* and in the traditional *zat pwe* also. It's unusual, but I was known for it. When I was young, I was sent abroad, I studied theatre in New York and Paris. When I came back, I'd been infected with the disease of America. In many of the performances I did, I began acting out the murders of the government instead of the murders of the gods. It increased my popularity dangerously. In the end I could only perform here in the mountains, in the theatre of the missing."

Loman said, "Which missing? Are there really American MIAs with Taksin?"

Auntie Soe patted Loman's knee. "Tell me what you understand."

"Very little. Sadong told me she was Taksin's spy. I know Aung Khin had me followed and either found that out, or he suspected it and used me to draw her out. Now he thinks to use her body to follow us to Taksin. You say that won't happen." Loman shrugged. "I know little else." The wind shifted again, the stink of the consequences of his ignorance, mixed with the sweet, cloying smell of opium, the smell of delirium, blew back into the cave. Loman told Auntie Soe about Mundy and Weyland, about Rangoon, the story Aung Khin had told him, pushing the mixed strands to this painted, shape-shifting, opium-kneading fate sitting in front of him, hoping Auntie Soe would weave it together for him. Auntie Soe heated more opium. He smoked and handed the pipe to Loman. Loman sucked in a lungful. He felt Sadong cringe.

"What about Sadong?" he asked. "Which story was true?"

"I don't know. Sadong would never tell me whether she was Khin's daughter or his lover or both. Perhaps she told Taksin. Taksin was the farthest place on earth to which she could flee from Khin. Some say she became Taksin's lover or daughter or both. And Taksin sent her back. What choice was there? Who could Taksin trust more to get information about Khin? But do you suppose, Loman, in the story Khin told you, that the rebel who fled to the jungle instructed his sister to go to the king, to share his bed so she could be her brother's spy? When she wrapped herself around her brother, did she stare into his eyes with malevolence, as if to say you'll never be rid of what you have done to me now? Do you think that was the real story, Loman?"

"If it is, Taksin truly will never forgive me."

Auntie Soe laughed. "Loman, you're an actor too in that bar where you hide like a spider, but which is really the prison you spun for yourself out of your own ass. But don't worry." He giggled and plucked at his clothing, his face changing, becoming feminine again. "Sadong was only a woman. You more than anyone should know how cheap the price of a woman, Loman."

As they came down the steep hillside, creepers and vines began to tunnel the path and the vegetation turned lush. Loman and Auntie Soe descended into a pocket of damp, miasmic air, heavy with the smell of mildew and rotting wood, an odor focused by the stench of Sadong's body. The valley in which Taksin's camp was hidden was a depression on a high plateau, a fold of trapped heat and vapors. It was a place, Loman imagined, that would be avoided by people used to the crystalline air of the mountains. For the last several miles, he and Auntie Soe had been stopped repeatedly by Taksin's watchers, the same scene played out each time: the bandolier-draped, wild-haired tribesmen or -women rising suddenly around them, smiling in greeting at Auntie Soe, then their eyes fleeing as if in embarrassment from the burden Loman carried. As they got closer, Loman felt Sadong's consciousness opening itself to the sights and smells.

They pushed through a bamboo picket that opened abruptly on a small sea of elephant grass. The blades cut at Loman's face and hands, and the flies that had formed a moving cloud around his burden went mad at the smell of fresh blood. The grass ended in a clearing ringed by sandbag bunkers, their bags torn, their sand leaking, and scarred by weedy trenches. Houses set on stilts, their roofs made of woven teak leaves, showed through the jungle on the fringes of the clearing. A pack of barking *pye* dogs ran out to greet them, whimpering as they caught the smell. Several naked, unhealthy-looking children, their stomachs ballooned with hunger, played quietly near a pond of green, scummy water. Loman saw only one small field, but the potatoes in it lay on top of the cracked earth, blackened, dried as gourds. More thatched-roof houses emerged into his focusing vision. They were strung out in the bush, maintaining an interval like experienced soldiers on patrol.

He noticed there were no cooking fires.

People started to emerge from the forest. As he and Auntie Soe passed, they gathered behind and formed a procession. When Auntie Soe stopped, Loman did also. He put down his weight, feeling it rip from his shoulders. The line of people gathered around, the ends coming together in a circle. There were turbaned and tattooed Shan men, some Lahu and Lisu, the multicolored stripes on the black-and-red vestlike shirts they wore reminding Loman of Seminole clothing; Hmongs, many young Burmese in worn, checkered *longyis* and khaki shirts; remnants, Loman guessed, of the democracy movement who had fled to the hills. But for the most part, standing out to his eyes, there were clusters of young women, their faces as heavily made up as Auntie Soe's, something off and satirical about the paint: eyeliner lines multiplied to masks of tiger stripes, fangs of bright red lipstick drawn below lower lips, green dot blush marks on cheeks, eyebrows bristling with black spikes. The women wore a mixture of cast-off military fatigues, tribal clothing, and tattered ragged city clothes. Some, Loman saw, wore scratched, faded number buttons. A teenaged girl, her lipstick smeared in a grotesque clown's smile over her mouth, cradled a large M-1 in her arms. They all stared at him with burning black eyes, as if the girls from his bar had followed or preceded him here, the others Auntie Soe had spoken of, girls who were there one day, gone the next, missing but not missed, replaced by other numbers. Not the MIAs but the dreams of soldiers gathered around him, plucked at his clothing, giggling mirthlessly at the expression on Loman's face.

Three women in tiger-striped fatigues, the only complete uniforms Loman had seen, were climbing down a bamboo ladder from a large, stilt-supported house next to a grove of pyinkado trees that intruded into the clearing. Auntie Soe put a hand on Loman's arm and squeezed. Loman stood still. The three turned and walked toward him.

"Taksin," Auntie Soe said unnecessarily.

The woman in the center was very tall and brittlely thin but walked with a brisk, bouncing stride, her focused energy swiveling heads around as though she were the memory of the beliefs they'd brought here. Loman saw she had drawn blood-red smears of lipstick down from the corners of her mouth, thick lines of black mascara exaggerating the slant of the eyes; red dashes, representations of cuts or tears, covered her cheeks. Loman didn't feel any particular surprise at the moment: he had half-expected it, from the way Auntie Soe had spoken, from the others here; he was in Jambudipa, the reversed planet.

Under the mask of makeup was the thin, intelligent face of

a woman perhaps in her fifties, her eyes bright with the anticipation of grief. She was chewing her lower lip; it was already, Loman saw, gnawed ragged. A stocky Lisu stepped in front of Loman and said something angrily. He unsheathed a kris knife and jabbed it at Loman's chest, the point clicking into his breastbone. He felt a trickle of blood run down his stomach. Auntie Soe said something in a soft, hissing voice. The Lisu stepped back, his eyes widening in fear. *Kohn Ahn Harm Kon Die*. Loman wondered suddenly how he was seen, spoken of in these hills; once he'd seen a poem in which a Vietnam veteran wondered if he was now the boogeyman with whom Vietnamese parents scared their children. The woman in the red slit skirt muttered and spit in the dust by Loman's feet.

Taksin spoke: a short, barked command. The murmuring that had been growing since they had stepped into the clearing stopped. It was very quiet. Taksin knelt by Sadong and unwrapped the blanket. The stench blasted out like heat from a stove.

The makeup on Taksin's face twitched in a grotesque dance, a mask coming to life. The Lisu who had prodded Loman wiped his eyes, and the painted women began a keening wail. Taksin raised her head. A howl exploded from her bloody lips.

She stopped. The two other women in jungle fatigues picked up Sadong and bore her away, the other women closing around them as they walked.

Taksin stood up slowly and looked into Loman's eyes. She licked her lips, swallowing blood.

"I've known since my outposts spotted you. But it's hard to see her like this, American, harder than I thought anything could be."

"I'm sorry."

"That means nothing to me."

Auntie Soe said something to her in Shan. She replied angrily. Loman had the sense his life was the focus of the argument. He felt detached from the debate. The voices rose and echoed around him. The fever pressed his skull with hot, wet hands. The argument continued. A man dressed as a woman arguing with a woman dressed as a man, here at the edge of the world.

An old woman was pressing a wet cloth against his face with an even, unrelenting pressure. She smiled at him. Her teeth were blackened by betel nut. The hut was lit by a kerosene lamp hung from a peg on the center pole. He was in the main room, divided from what he supposed were the sleeping rooms by a thatch partition; his back was propped uncomfortably against it. When he shifted and looked through the weave, he saw girls, their faces made up with the same grotesque swirls and mixes of color, lying on the straw matting, clinging to each other in an uneasy sleep. Loman's ears rang; he had passed out or slept, but he had no memory of the transition to the room. He saw he'd been dressed in clean khaki trousers and a green T-shirt. The clothing seemed new.

"You can thank Khin for your garments," Taksin said. She was sitting hunched on a low stool, in the shadows, pulling a tent of her lip up between her teeth. "A caravan we ambushed turned out to be going into Burma instead of coming out. We expected opium, but the mules were all carrying clothing to be sold in the Lashio black market. We have no food in the camp, but there are new clothes for whoever wishes."

He touched the T-shirt. Who could Taksin trust more to get information about Khin, Auntie Soe had said. "Did Sadong tell you about the caravans? Khin must hate your guts—how much have you been hitting him?"

"Not enough," Taksin muttered.

A girl in a white sleeveless T-shirt, a scratched red massage parlor button pinned on it, was sitting behind the old woman. She leaned forward and pushed a black-lacquer bowl in front of Loman, the soup in it smelling strongly of lemon grass. He put a hand on her wrist to stop her.

"You had better drink something," Taksin said.

Loman touched the button. "Where are these girls from?"

"Tea or rice wine?"

He realized his mouth and throat were aching with dryness. "Tea."

The old woman shook her head, yes, and smiled at Loman again, pleased at understanding him. "Tea," she repeated triumphantly. She waved at the charcoal brazier in the center of the room. The girl ducked back to it, keeping her head lower than Taksin's in respect. She handed the cup to the old woman, who gave it to Loman.

She patted his face as he drank.

"She's Lahu," Taksin said, as if it explained everything. "You seem to have a way with primitives and women, don't you, Loman? I'm sure your girls saw you more as a father than a pimp."

"Which did Sadong see you as?" Loman said.

Taksin closed her eyes and opened them, nodding.

"Was she really Khin's daughter?" he asked.

Taksin shuddered. A slight smile played on her lips. "Such information is confidential," she said. "Careless dissemination breaks the trust relationship."

Loman looked at her. "I'll have that wine now."

"Yes, of course."

She called something to the girl, who left the room and came back with a small porcelain bottle. The wine was harsh and warming. The old woman shrilly said something.

"She said to be careful, your urine was reddish," Taksin said.

"What does that mean?"

The woman replied to Taksin's question in a long, musical sentence. Taksin smiled.

"She doesn't know. Only that it should be yellow."

The smile disappeared, the face flowing back into a configuration of grief like water filling deep ruts.

The room pressed in on Loman, the faces of the three women, old, young, bitter, advanced and retreated.

"Why do you call yourself Taksin?" he asked.

"Oh, perhaps Auntie Soe inspired me; he was a great pwe player. When we came to the forest, we all took names; it was a joke between us, to confuse the authorities. Or perhaps to confuse the forest. Or perhaps that's not how you meant the question. Perhaps you were asking if I'm perverse."

"I own a bar in Bangkok. I don't know what to call perverse."

Her outlined eyes prismed the lamplight.

"The perverse exists," she said, her voice toneless. "It hungers. It feeds. It grows. With a man like Khin to whom control of the external is necessary to achieve release of the internal, the pattern is predictable. As usual in these cases, 'Sadong,' " she spoke the name as if in quotation marks, "the victim child, was completely dependent upon the father figure: as long as she was in his orbit, the acts he made her do, or did to her, were within custom. Nothing contradicted. Education was at home, by tutor. The male need for perfect control was perfectly achieved. Thus when she was allowed to go to university, to the outside world, she discovered the personal revulsion she felt was not a sickness. Her father sensed her disgust. She became involved in the democracy movement, projecting her own need for liberation. When the movement was destroyed, some of her friends in it came to join me."

Loman stared at her, this mask-painted middle-aged woman in jungle fatigues, sitting in a house of stilts speaking psychobabble.

"She didn't come?"

"Eventually. At first she was arrested. Her father got her out of Burma and set her up in Bangkok, in the Hotel Miami. He tried to return her safely inside himself, as it were. She came to me from there. She was confused, extremely vulnerable. In pain. Like any of my girls."

"And you made her go back to him."

She shook her head. "Yes," she said. "I couldn't have Khin's daughter here. I fed her back to him. How many girls did you feed back to men's dreams, Loman? In your Bangkok bar?"

Sadong burned inside him, a sudden, twisting knot of pain, a taste of betrayal that rose in his throat and mouth, bitter as bile.

"They all depend on me," Taksin whispered. "Was her pain worse than theirs? Imagine being put on the market, by the parental figure. I couldn't put my other clients at risk. Any interruption of the healing process we'd begun would be traumatic and irreversible." She looked troubled, her words trailing. "There was of course the moral aspect. But I have to think that Sadong understood. She heard things, Loman, in the hotel, at her father's house, where she had promised herself never to return. She did it for me, for all of us here, for our survival and wholeness." She caught her lip between her teeth again, as if to stop her words.

Neither of them spoke. In the silence something nagged at Loman like the memory of a promise.

"What about the MIAs?" he asked.

Taksin smiled at him.

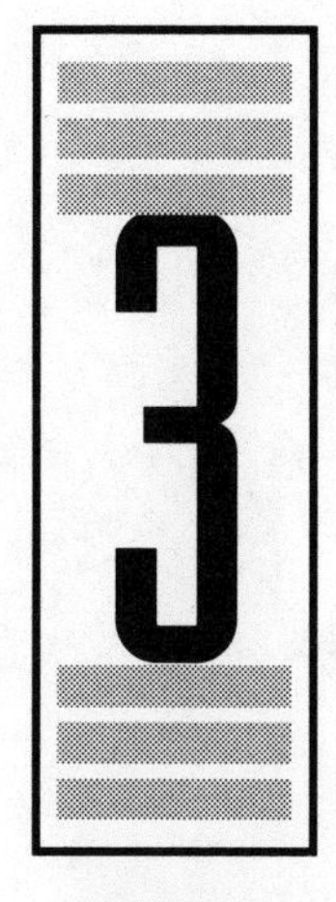

NAT PWE

Nap time, nat time; hi brother. Come on in, the ether's fine. Visit the void. Welcome to the Hotel Nat. Fingernail dancers with coldly glittering eyes. Scarecrow devas with scarred necks and two faces. Jambudipa in Miniature. The Mount Meru Theme Park. Your guide, sister Sadong. Or maybe I'm nothing. Is this me, or is this memory? The last microdot of a drug that once got under your skin. A figment. Someone you ate. Your own mind, casting out in its anxious sleep, pulling out a thread here, a strand there, weaving together. Why not? Is there any difference between that and what you called Sadong before? An image of a woman, loosening and tightening a longyi. Inviting in, shutting out. A coherence just out of reach.

What a drag.

Do you want to know what it's like to be a nat?

It is twilight. When the solidity of the day is called into doubt. When smell and sound and sight and touch and taste and thought, the six ayatana that distort the world, soften and mingle. Twilight people wrapped in longyis twitter to each other, glide by like dark notes of music. Tone, tone, three-quarter tone, three-quarter tone, tone, three-quarter tone, three-quarter tone. The glow of charcoal fires shows through their skins. They waver as I pass through them. I feel them as flickers in my blood. There are no men or women or things. All is no longer merely an interplay of ayatana, sense bases. The need the senses place on the being to narrow the world to their restrictions. I see what the human eye cannot see. I see the dreams of men and women hovering over them as unformed souls and beasts and fabulous monsters. I see the guardian chinthes of pagodas roaring at me as I fly overhead. I see other beings suffering in lower planes of existence. I see the guardian spirits of forests and mountains. I see through both physical barriers and barriers of time. It's a trip.

Come with me. We'll turn a corner of time. I know you don't want to see this now, but you must. We join now more seamlessly than we ever could in life. I weave me into you. I'm your nat sister. Come with me. I am in the house where I grew up, a house woven of white flowers. The walls of my room are cunningly fashioned of luminous white petals. At sunset the night grows into the skins of the petals and turns them black. They rustle and fold softly around me, hold me gripped gently in their center. Their fragrance permeates my skin, hides the beckoning musk, the ripening odors of my body. They knit the heavy silk of a plant's sleep into my brain. Their fibers wrap around my veins, rustle in the spaces between my bones. My skin grows into their living flesh. Who can find me?

He can.

At night he comes looking, stalking the hallways. At night his hands convulse and change the way a caress changes to a pinch. Moonlight slides under his skin like a thin silver knife. Moonlight enters his soft eyes, turns them hard as pearls. At night his nails grow into long, curved claws, their undersides black with blood. His teeth grow pointed and sharp as fangs. His smooth skin erupts and bristles with hair. At night the smile of love twists into a gape of hunger. He tears through petal walls. He holds and shreds and pierces as the stinger of a bee plunges and rips with blind need. But by morning the room grows around me again from its bud, a hard ache at the center of my body. All day it grows, thickening around me, frantically drawing in the sunlight, desperately shining with bright colors. All the while quivering with the knowledge that night would come. As relentlessly, as inevitably, as the footsteps I heard behind me when I left you at the Shwedagon.

He climbed down the bamboo ladder into day. A sharp, sweet smell of cooked meat hung thickly in the air; heavy snakes of smoke, pressed close to the ground by the humidity, wrapped around the trunks and lower branches of the pyinkado trees. He became aware of Taksin watching him. Her stare prodded out a picture of his first view of the camp, the absence of cooking fires, and he realized, feeling sick, from where the smoke must have come.

"We cremated her while you slept," Taksin said.

"You should have waited for me." He felt a strange anger at not having been there.

"It doesn't matter."

The line of tribespeople, Burmese students, and Taksin's girls waiting in the yellow dust parted, and he saw the source of the smoke and the smell, a black oblong cylinder of ashes on top of a cairn of stones, still held by a seared cage of bones, the blackened skull grinning at him. For an instant he was looking at himself, his insides yanked out raw and laid in the sun.

He turned away. Auntie Soe was squatting with a circle of

men and women to the right of Sadong's corpse, all of them smoking small, tightly rolled Shan cheroots. He looked up at Loman and offered a cheroot.

"It will help mask the stink," he said.

He lit it, sucked in, and offered it again. Loman could smell its smoke now, the resinous sweetness of the opium mixed with the tobacco. He took it and inhaled deeply. A flute trilled a playful bright dance of music in the air.

The man behind Auntie Soe had a thirteen-string Burmese harp cradled in his lap. His blunt, callused fingers caressed the buffalo-hide hull, the gilt curve of the prow, fluttered over the strings. The music drifted with the wind trembling the pyinkado leaves over his head, one sound naming the other in some place beneath words. The smoke pushed in his head. One of the other men, a Shan, his skin tattooed with the fierce fanged faces of animistic deities, sat in front of a large *patt ma* drum. He began tapping it gently, the beat taken up and added to in intricate riffs by a woman hitting a bamboo clapper. Another woman, a wizened Lahu lady in a red-and-yellow striped tunic, her ears stretched by silver, puffed her cheeks and blew the *palwe*, the bamboo flute, again, swaying to the hollow, lonely notes. The painted girls swayed with the sound, moaning. The discordant music jumbled into a kind of wildness in Loman's head, a wildness that tumbled and curled with the tendrils of smoke.

Auntie Soe leapt to his feet and began to dance. The coins on his vest jingled in rhythm. His feet and wrists bent to impossible angles. As Loman watched, he transformed, his eyes glowing golden, his face suffused with terrible hunger, his body stalking, deadly, muscles tensed and ready to spring, and then his face twitching with fear and panic, his steps mincing, delicate, ready to take flight, his body trembling. He was the stalking tiger; he was the tiger's prey. He straightened and became human. He was male. He walked a step, changed imperceptibly. She was female. It was a demonstration of his powers, a prelude, Loman sensed. *Nat pwe,* Sadong whispered, Taksin whispered, their voices weaving in the notes of the flute, inside his head; this is the forbidden performance, the pwe never seen. The drum beat faster, the flute and clapper rhythm winding around it, something like hands inside Loman wringing tighter and tighter. A moan leaked from his lips, joined with the moans spilling from the mouths of the circling people, from the distorted, painted mouths of the girls. He felt their years rotting into him like something carried on his shoulders. *Nat pwe.* The music poured out of the harp, wrapped with the cloying stink in his nostrils. Auntie Soe brought his face close to Loman's and convulsed it into the panicked face of a woman being chased by a tiger's hunger, chased by Loman, chased by Khin down the corridors of a seedy hotel; inside him Sadong screamed and Auntie Soe was a young girl cringing in her bed, feeling the terror of the kind, strong hands of the daylight, the father's hands, shifting, changing, touching, grabbing; Loman felt her writhe and shrink inside him, her terror soiling him to the soul. Then Auntie Soe's face fell apart and reformed into a mask creased with self-disgust and need; it was Loman's own face, the twist of hunger, the intent, beer-gut thrust of his body, hips pumping the air frantically, erection tenting out: he chased himself in circles, humped the air, the features changing as an eye winks: a face that twisted and bit at itself. Loman felt the tears coursing down his cheeks; he watched them stream down Auntie Soe's mirroring face.

Taksin was beside him, her mouth pressed to his ear.

This is the nat pwe, the forbidden pwe, Sadong whispered in his head.

"This is the dance after Anawrahta," Taksin whispered in his ear. "In the dance of the *pwe*, the *pya zat*, there are certain new traditional characters, in our new tradition. The first is the king who would rule the day and the night, who would bind the chaos of dreams. The Red Naga."

The harp twanged discordantly; Auntie Soe's eyes hardened with cynicism, a sneer curled his lips. His movements became serpentine—a sinuous stalking. Weyland winked suddenly out of Auntie Soe's features.

"Now enter Lord Bent, the traitor nat," Taksin announced. "The Devourer." She waved her hand and the drum beat a flat, menacing staccato and Auntie Soe danced Khin, unmistakably Khin, squat, striding, his broad flat face intent and concentrated beyond evil, a force as strong and simple and terrible with need as a force of nature.

"Now Prince Handsome of the Fortunate Kingdom."

The flute trilled playfully. Auntie Soe's face smoothed, Khin's face turning in on itself, concentration spilling off into simplicity: Loman saw Elliott Mundy skipping happily, beaming with vulnerable openness, his face alight and boyish.

"Our *pwe* is this," Taksin said. "The Red Naga seeks to entice to his service a nat of his own with whom he can subjugate the wild nats of the mountains. He chooses not Sakka, as the old Anawrahta chose, but Lord Bent. Lord Bent, the nat of *pamada*, of the poison of forgetfulness, of immersion in the senses." The drum beat. Khin sulked in the circle, plucking invisible flowers, his face lit with malevolence. "The Red Naga," Khin stopped, smiled, twitched into Weyland, "goes back to the Fortunate Kingdom, floats into the dreams of Prince Handsome. His plan is to use the prince to ensnare Lord Bent, but first he ensnares the prince with tales of prisoners held in magic spells, frozen into the shapes of trees. He whispers to the prince that Lord Bent's *pamada* is destroying the Fortunate Kingdom, a hero is needed to stop the wickedness." Mundy's face emerged, looked about happily; the flute trilled. "How? the prince asks." The harp twanged. Weyland leaned forward, whispering, rubbing his hands together. "Ah, the Red Naga says, Lord Bent also drifts in the current of *kamogha*, which is desire, lust, and attachment. And in the Fortunate Kingdom, he reminds the prince, delightful objects grow on trees." Taksin's tongue touched Loman's ear; Loman started, turned to see her bitten lips twist into a smile, her stare fastening him. "This nat, he whispers to the prince, can be bought."

The three instruments sounded at once, the music crescendoing, growing more and more frantic as Mundy skipped boyishly to a pyinkado tree and stripped shiny leaves from it, then hopped exuberantly around the clearing, throwing leaves, Auntie Soe's face twitching as he sank to his knees and rose again as Khin, Lord Bent chasing after, scooping the leaves with sly, leering greed and then the face shifting again, ever so slightly to Weyland, following behind Mundy, his hands raised, his fingers fluttering, jerking strings, a puppeteer's fingers. The audience held its sides and laughed at the comic figures chasing leaves, grabbing at each other's behinds.

"The Red Naga whispers into his prince's ear," Taksin whispered into Loman's ear. "He can arrange anything. He can grant him three wishes. He can give him eternal life. All that is needed is to perform *akusala*, deeds."

Weyland beamed and nodded and spun into Khin, into Mundy, the faces swimming, the crowd laughing, clapping in delight, the dance going in larger circles.

"Fuck fairy tales," Loman said. "Tell me what's going on."

There was a flurry of drum rolls, a jangle of cords, and the music stopped.

Taksin nodded, gnawing her lip. There were spots of blood, Loman saw, on her yellowed teeth. "Fuck fairy tales," she repeated. "The pwe is this. Mundy thinks to make a preemptive buy from Khin. It's an idea Weyland put into his head. He thinks he is buying Khin: he apparently feels that this is a good way to stop opium from coming into the United

States. He apparently believes that it is the price for the MIAs Khin claims to know about. For Us."

Loman remembered the feeling of Sadong's stiff fingers, slipping under his blindfold, her nails raking his face, trying to open his eyes. "That's crazy," he said.

"Yes," Taksin agreed. "Both ideas."

"Khin doesn't even control the entire crop," Loman said.

"Not while I'm here, sitting on his caravan lines," Taksin said. Khin stopped, planted his feet apart. He stared at Taksin with hatred. "Though even if I didn't exist, there are others, and he won't sell everything he has to Mundy anyway. Why should he? He will sell part of it, a good amount, and market the rest as usual. No, not as usual. At a higher price. Due to scarcity."

Loman stared at her. "Mundy has to understand that."

"Mundy will have a pile of bundles to burn, and some of them may even contain opium. Mundy believes what he wishes to believe. He wishes to believe the missing will arise like the phoenix from the ashes of that fire." Her hand waved, conjured a whirlwind of ash.

"And Weyland?"

She pointed at Auntie Soe, now the foolish young prince again, eyes wide, chewing leaves. Mundy's face trickled away; Weyland's leer claimed it. He danced for Loman, leaping back and forth.

"Weyland wishes to create a fact and present it as a gift that will have to be used," Taksin said. "Weyland wants a part in the *pwe* again, for himself, for his country."

What we're about, Weyland had said, turns out to be entertainment.

Auntie Soe danced in circles.

"Again?"

Taksin giggled, her eyes bright, her face twitching the lines of paint on it. A trail of drool and blood from her torn lip spilled from the corner of her mouth. She licked at it. "Listen," she said. "He was here before, Loman."

"I know."

"Did you know he ran Khin before, for the Americans, financed his army and operations?"

Loman shook his head slowly. "No. But I thought he'd probably be connected in some way."

"Connected," she said merrily. "It was how he started his career. Khin was his star. You understand how it was: the Americans still thought the Kuomintang could be used against the Chinese communists. They thought they could be involved in interesting times."

"I know the history," Loman said.

"And has it made you free?"

The drum beat like a pulse in his head.

"How the hell do you know all this?"

Her eyes widened mockingly. "Oh, I have . . . connections also. And I've known Weyland, Loman, I've known him a long time." She touched the remains, her hand groping blindly in the ashes as if seeking connection. A startled look crossed her face, as if she'd found it. Her face went blank. She smiled at Loman. "I didn't know he was getting involved with Khin again. Not until now. If baby had told me, I would have never let her do what she did. But she was very careful, communicating with me; we kept strict radio discipline, it wasn't time yet for our next contact. It wasn't time." Her eyes brimmed suddenly.

Loman stopped her hand.

The flute's melody thickened into a kind of yearning.

Loman shook his head. "I can believe Weyland wants an Asian army to play with again. But I have a hard time believing the American Congress or administration is condoning or financing this kind of operation. Not even Langley," he added.

Auntie Soe did the three monkeys; each had Loman's face.

"Official funds would not have to be used, you see," Taksin said softly, as if she were puzzling it out for herself. "There are groups of interested citizens that would pay millions if they thought Khin had even one MIA: there's much money available for anyone who can produce the missing; that's why Weyland had to make them up: they ache through too many nights like a phantom pain. You above all should know that, *Kon Ahn Harm Kon Die.*"

She looked down at her ashy hand as if startled, picked it up and waved at her own people. They smiled at her dreamily, nodding. They were hanging on her words, spoken in a language they didn't understand, as if they were the mutterings of an oracle. "Why do you think the Burmese government sent someone to speak to you in Rangoon?"

"I'm not sure he was a government representative."

"Are you that stupid? The man you met in the Inye Lake Hotel, as you described him, made a point of showing you he was official. Connected. The Burmese are scared; they knew you were sent by Mundy and Weyland; they must have known of their feelers to Aung Khin, they have agents in Bangkok. As far as they were concerned, you were an official American representative going to offer American backing to a rebel force. They know their history too. But they hoped that when you knew that they knew, you would tell your superiors that the operation was compromised and it would be called off. They could have prevented you from going, but it would have just delayed matters. They chose to be subtle."

"*Anandeh,*" Loman said.

The drum echoed the three syllables of the word. Taksin got to her feet and spread her arms out and spun, her eyes tightly closed.

"Weyland gives people what they want, Loman. They

want the missing, he provides. They want an end to the plague of drugs, he shows them how. They want a trip north, a chance for redemption. Why not? And if they want you, if you're the price, he gives them you."

He felt Sadong swirl into him, a taste of ashes that thickened in his throat like grief. "You're saying Weyland knew that Khin was using me to finger Sadong?"

Taksin stopped. She opened her eyes. "To finger?" She seemed to find the phrase interesting. She extended her forefinger and tapped his forehead with it. "Think. Think as Khin would think, Loman. He is being offered the world. America is going to back him as it did before, even to sending the same man. If his ambition is to stay with the drug trade, then he can wipe out all his opposition. If it is larger, who knows how far he can go? If Weyland wishes to play kingmaker, he'll be glad to play the king. But then there was me. Undermining him. Hitting his caravans. Interfering with business. How would it all look to the Americans? Would they change their minds? And how did I know where his caravans would go? There must be spies in his organization. Perhaps he even knows or suspects his daughter is the one. But he has to be sure. He thinks," she said, tapping his forehead again, "if Weyland wishes to dance a pwe about the missing to his congressman, why not? But instead of the two of them coming directly to his camp, he suggests a deepening of the drama. Send a representative instead. A pimp who wouldn't know he's pimping. He'll even help, he tells Weyland. He'll dress up some *farang* mule like an MIA, like a pimp's dream, to lure the pimp north."

"You still can't be sure Khin told Weyland how he wanted to use me," Loman said.

"Is it that important to you?"

"I need to know the truth."

"It won't free you either. But no, I can't be sure," she admitted. "Khin might not have told Weyland why he wanted you to come. He might have simply insisted on having a messenger sent. It doesn't matter if Weyland knew how you were being used or not. It only mattered to Khin that someone was being sent. That you would come, to draw out spies, to point the way to us. Then Khin visits his daughter. He tells her of Mundy, of the coming meeting with Mundy's representative that will take place in, say, a month, maybe more; he tells her how he will be king of the nats. With American power behind him, American weaponry, money, technology, he will crush Taksin, he tells her. Crush this little female mischief nat nipping at him. He knows that if she is my spy, if there's any doubt in his mind, this will test and condemn her. He knows she will have to act to save me. And so she contacts you. Here is what I think she did, Loman. She sends the two *farangs* to you, they ask you to come to me. She thinks, my Sadong, that her father will assume that Weyland and Mundy are sending out feelers to me, that they want to play me against Khin, back me, his competition, and that will sabotage the agreement."

"For Christ's sake, how would he know what they asked me to do—did he have people looking over our shoulders in the bar?"

She sighed at his slowness. "No. He had Sadong. His spy. She only had to report to him that two *farangs* connected to Taksin met with you. She only had to have you come, act it out to back up her story. You only had to move through the scene like a puppet, representing actions whose meanings you didn't know. But Khin lied. He knew Weyland was coming to you right away. And you decided to play both roles, one for her and the Japanese and the Australian, one for Weyland. So she had to go to you in Rangoon, try to stop you, have you come to me instead of her father."

He shook his head. "I don't believe Khin would risk his meeting with Mundy and Weyland just to set up his daughter."

She looked at him wonderingly. "Then it isn't truth you want, Loman—it's innocence. Are you still that American? He risks nothing. Either he did it with Weyland's knowledge. Or he simply thinks he'll eliminate her, and me, and then deal with Mundy anyway. From an even stronger position."

Loman snapped, "You want your own innocence, Taksin. If you knew Khin was trying to expose her, why didn't you warn her?"

Taksin closed her eyes. "Loman, I sent her back to her father; I have no illusion of innocence. But I didn't know about Weyland, about her plans. Not then. All of this is conjecture, after the fact." She waved at the fact lying before them. Her hand was trembling. She looked at it, brought her finger forward and touched his forehead again. Fingered him. "Think of it, Loman. He had the meeting on film. He saw his daughter's act of betrayal. It gave him an excuse to wipe out the negative self-definition caused by Sadong's actions forcing him to acknowledge his abuse of her." She got up and stood by Sadong, her stare fixed to Loman, her teeth gnawing at her lower lip, as if to punish it for the stream of jargon that had suddenly escaped. She patted the bones tenderly.

"What did you mean, I pointed the way to you?" Loman felt the heat of her touch linger on his skin, a hot coin pressed between his eyes. "Auntie Soe lost his trackers."

Auntie Soe stopped. He looked down at his feet. The drum beat slowed and stopped. The clearing went silent, though it seemed to be spinning around Loman as if he were a pivot, the red-hot coin on his forehead its center.

"Auntie Soe has many talents. As you see. But Auntie Soe is an artist. He is not acquainted with the power of American technology. The power Weyland will give to his nat. Do you think the pwe is over, Loman? For us, the end of the pwe will be Khin," Taksin said. "We stand between him and a perfect world."

She plunged her hand into Sadong's chest, her fingers digging and clawing. There was a cracking, splintering sound. She drew her hand back slowly, her ash-whitened fingers pinching something metallic and gleaming between them, like the magic egg of Sadong's soul.

"The end will be Khin," she said again, and threw the object down. She raised her foot and crushed it under her heel. The flute wailed. The harp jangled. Taksin laughed and leapt next to Auntie Soe. The two of them danced for Loman, their faces and forms fluid as dreams in the shadows of the trees.

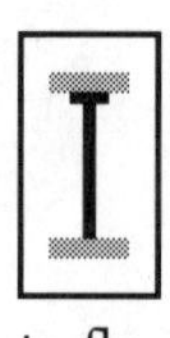he transmission from Loman came on Monday of the second week. Weyland came out of the hootch, staring at the coordinates he'd written on a scrap of paper, waving a map at Harry. Telling him it was time to fly.

They had spent the time getting the aircraft in shape and inventorying the equipment Weyland had stored in the hut near the landing zone. Harry couldn't understand why they couldn't simply get the coordinates from Aung Khin, fly in, get it over. He hadn't bought what Weyland explained to him about Wireless Willy. For a guy with a phobia about radios, Khin seemed to go for electronics: the cases the red man was going to bring to him were filled with spook gadgetry.

At first it had gone slowly. He had feared Al or Chuckie would try to get back at Weyland, but who they got at was Harry, he was teacher's monitor, refusing to take him seriously when he'd insisted on showing them the rudimentaries of pre-flighting and crewing the UH-1 Iroqouis. All bullshit could do when you flung it in the air was fall, no matter how much you wanted it to hover, he told them. They grew silent, resentful of his seriousness, like kids pissed at another kid who had suddenly grown up.

Once he'd gotten them to work, though, they got into the ritual of it as he'd thought they would: the three of them, and Mundy too, joining them, tightening something that was as much against Weyland as between themselves.

And when he at last flew, the panic he had feared thrilled through him: a sudden and terrible awareness of the madly whirling chaos of slashing blades, the centrifugal urge of dispersal of thousands of dancing pieces each trying to tear off on its own crazed spin into the void. He saw himself dancing before chaos like a crazed shaman, feet pumping the pedals, left hand twisting the collective and throttle, right delicately twirling the cyclic stick until he felt the balance of pitch and torque, of push and pull, and yaw slide into place, align with a center in his own heart.

"Charon, this is Barkeep," Loman's voice crackled in his earphones, as startling as a dead man's voice coming out of the void.

"Come in, Barkeep."

He listened to what Loman wanted him to do, then keyed his mike again.

"You in trouble, Jake?" he'd asked. "You need an extract?"

It took him a few seconds to recognize the noise in his earphones as laughter.

He swung on to the new course Loman had given him, flying north for about half an hour, then west for another fifteen minutes. He checked the map again, and looked back into the compartment. Weyland was leaning out of the hatch, peering intently at the jungle. Harry turned to the left, so he could come in out of the sun.

A voice crackled in his earphones. "Charon, I'm marking the zone."

As Loman popped the flare, he remembered that red was the signal for enemy in the area. He hadn't, he didn't think, recalled that when he had chosen the color as his signal, but he didn't suppose he would change it now if he could. The flare hissed up and exploded; its ruby star drifted down, swinging under the small chute. Before it touched the ground he heard a vague sound that evolved into a pulse beating somewhere beyond the veil of sky. The noise grew into the familiar *whop-whop* of helicopter rotors, the sound and the arc and fall of the flare and now the red dirt stinging his eyes and face, an event corded back in his history or maybe a notion of what he thought his history should be; Loman no longer knew.

The helicopter was a tan Huey with no markings. Loman looked up to see his customers coming to him: Helicopter Harry, his face framed by a helmet, in the right, pilot's seat: there was no copilot. Chuckie's-in-Love was sitting in the crew chief's seat, behind an M-60. He leaned out and gave Loman a thumbs-up, tilting too far forward so that he slipped and a pair of hands, Fat Al's, reached out and pulled him safely back into the cargo bay. Loman could see Mundy and Weyland leaning forward on their bench, squinting down at him intently.

He waved and tried to look friendly. He had assumed that Weyland had never been to Khin's camp and that the initial appearance of the landing zone would convince him he was in the right place. If not, Weyland could still just say a word into the intercom to Harry and abort. Loman tried not to think about what would happen if he did: Taksin had every gun in the camp trained on the ship. Over the last two days, she had taken to fits of unprovoked laughter. He had the feeling she would just as soon have everything end in a helicopter crash and a crispy congressman as try Loman's half-baked plan.

The helicopter landed. Mundy hopped out first, his eyes wide, consuming the jungle, the camp, the armed tribesmen. He beamed his congressman's smile at Loman and ran forward in a Groucho shuffle, ducking his head to avoid the rotors while extending his hand as if he were coming onto a factory floor to touch flesh with the voters. The bumbling young prince running into his character in the pwe as he came out of the whir of noise toward Loman. Weyland jumped out after him, the Red King in baggy khaki pants and shirt, stumbling as the inertia took him forward, scrambling after the impulsive young hero. The audience, Taksin's strange mix of students, hill people, and whores, emerging from its place in the forest, tittered appreciatively under the rotor noise. Weyland slowed down, a faint puzzlement creasing his forehead.

Loman waved at Harry, making an up-and-away gesture. The helicopter shot up as if released. Loman saw Fat Al and Chuckie framed in the bay, both of them grinning, taking pictures of their MIA mission.

When there was nothing but the silence and the jungle, a slow look of comprehension opened on Weyland's face. He cursed and reached into his pocket, but Auntie Soe stepped up next to him and pointed an AK-47 with one hand. He brought a finger to his lips and shook his head at Weyland, No-no. Weyland withdrew his hand.

The old woman played a few high, laughing notes on the *palwe* flute.

Loman reached into Weyland's pocket. He pulled out a rectangular metal box: an emergency signal beacon. He put it into his own pocket.

"What the fuck is this, Loman?" Weyland said.

Some of the girls, giggling, mimicked the white man's anger with nostalgic delight: *wha da fuk, wha da fuk, Lo-man.* Taksin's people had closed in around them now. Mundy started to work the crowd. "Hello, hello, it's good to see you," he said. "Representative Elliott Mundy here." The girls looked at him with their smeared, unforgiving faces. A skeletal fifteen-year-old with track marks on her arms, two purple and green spiders—glittering with sparkles—on her cheeks, playfully prodded him in the groin with the butt of an M-1. Mundy's smile wavered.

Taksin called out something sharply. She came through the crowd, her thin plant height swaying, her two tiger-striped factotums striding behind her. Mundy beamed at her in relief, but it turned to uncertainty as he saw the designed blotch of her face makeup, her eyes. Taksin smiled back at him and said something low and musical in Shan. The two bodyguards seized Mundy's arms. Taksin reached out and seized his face between her hands. She pushed in hard on both sides of Mundy's face, bringing her own face closer, staring as if a sickness or her own death had been given eyes into which she could stare. Mundy's eyes darted back and forth, as if trying to look for a way to get out of his head.

"Who are you?" he stammered.

"The wicked dyke of the east," Weyland said. "Hello Miss Dawee."

Taksin let go of Mundy and turned to Weyland. "How terrible to see you again, Weyland," she said.

"My pleasure, Dawee."

She smiled pleasantly. "If you call me that again, I'll kill you."

"I believe you would too, partner," Weyland said affably. "Fact, I believe you will anyway."

"Who is this person, Weyland?" Mundy said.

"Why don't you tell me you demand to know, congressperson? I've been waiting to see how that phraseology works out, in the jungle." Weyland smiled and nodded, opening his hands. "Congressperson, this, dah-dah, is Taksin, of song and story. I knew her in Bangkok and Chiang Mai once when she was the very rich Dr. D— Ph.D." He pinched his lips together, cutting off the rest of the name, smiling merrily at Taksin, their eyes locked. "The working girl's friend." He looked around contemptuously at the ragged camp, Taksin's starved little army of misfits. Loman felt a rise of offense at his stare that surprised him, as if these people had become his own. Weyland's gaze fell on him.

"Hello, barkeep," he said. "Who do you think you are today?"

"The famous barking dog."

He nodded. "Who warns of approaching tigers. How'd you get here from there, Loman? Or you plan to come to this lady from the get-go?"

"You can't get here from there," Loman said.

Weyland shrugged. "Okay, you got me, now what you going to do with me?" He smiled at Mundy, who was staring at both of them like a child waiting to be let into the adults' conversation. "You have some kind of hostage situation in mind? I doubt Khin would go for it. He'd just figure we'd come to deal with Taksin." A startled look opened his face; he shook his head as if at his own thickness. "Clever lady. That was the idea, wasn't it? That's what you and good yeoman Loman are on about."

"Weyland, will you please tell me what in the hell is going on?" Mundy demanded. His eyes were wide as a fawn's. Taksin had let go of his face, but panic was still squeezing his features. He had flown into an idea and it had turned into heat and jungle and strange little people with an agenda of their own. "Weyland," Mundy said, "you will tell me what is happening and you will get us out of here. The situation does not seem to be in control."

Weyland laughed.

"I don't find what I said amusing."

"Congressperson, I find you endlessly amusing. You are a source of never-ending joy for me."

"You son of a bitch, tell me what is going on."

Weyland explained slowly, as to a child. "We're here so we can't go to Khin. Khin will think we've decided to deal with Taksin. That's why good buddy Loman brought us here, to put that bee in the big Kahuna's poppy. Either that, or Taksin here's just going to kill us. That right, Taksin? I leave anything out?"

"I don't understand," Mundy said.

"That's a whole way of life for you, isn't it, congressperson?"

The jungle at the north end of the clearing seemed to part slightly, discharge two small brown men in loin cloths, then close after them. Their bodies were covered with blue snake tattoos, chests and arms and thighs encased in scaly coils. The two glided toward the center in an elusive, stroboscopic slither, so that Loman had the sensation of not being able to verify they were really there. It was the feeling he had had with Sadong. *Phi Thong Luang*, Yellow Leaf Ghosts; Taksin, Loman understood, used the little folk as scouts. The two men were on either side of her now, whispering, their voices had the sibilance of rustling leaves. Taksin's face hardened under its paint as they spoke into her ears.

The people working on the perimeter defenses—filling sandbags, digging the trenches deeper, stringing wire—had seen the scouts arrive. Now they drew in toward the center of Taksin, Auntie Soe, and the two scouts like filings to a magnet. Loman looked at the weapons they carried, categorizing them, an old habit: M-1s, Enfields, M-3 submachine guns, BARs, some M-14s. He had seen an M-60 in one of the sandbag emplacements around the clearing, another had a

Browning .50 caliber, but there were no mortars, no rocket launchers, nothing that could match what he had seen in Khin's camp.

"The Ghosts say it will take Khin about four days to get here," Weyland said, appearing at Loman's side. He was smiling, listening to the conversation. "Apparently he's not taking the same route you took."

Since yesterday, Taksin had let Weyland and Mundy wander unconfined: they were watched, but there was no place to go. Loman suspected that she still wasn't sure whether to kill them out of revenge or try to deal with them. He wasn't sure which he had wanted when he had given her the idea, offered, for that matter, to call them in on her radio, use the frequency he had been given. He had only known he wanted them here, with him, for a change stuck in the consequences of their plans.

Mundy, for the most part, sat by himself staring at the people and at the jungle, waiting to wake up. But Weyland strode around the camp with a proprietary smile, sitting in, smoking and eating with the groups of Burmese students, the Lahu, Lisu, Hmongs, Kachins, even the Thai girls, joking with each group in their own language. At first the people in the camp had stayed aloof, but Loman saw they were impressed and flattered.

"What I don't understand," Weyland said, "is why she doesn't just hat out. This base, she's only been here a month I'm told, barkeep. It's what I figured; that's how she's survived Khin up to now. By staying fluid."

In his way, Loman thought, Weyland was a greater shapeshifter than either *pwe* player Auntie Soe or politician Mundy; he didn't recognize the man he'd met in Bangkok. Weyland was fluid. He had seen Taksin looking after Weyland, chewing her tattered lip. When she caught Loman's gaze she smiled sardonically at him as if to say, you see. He had expected a scene, but she just seemed to press each burst of laughter from her people at Weyland's jokes into herself like a thorn, smile and retreat more deeply into her silence. The people had looked after her uneasily. But her sulk hadn't drawn them away from Weyland.

The only time Loman saw Taksin nearly lose it was when Weyland flirted with some of her girls. They had only looked at him stonily, but underneath they were cool and amused. After a time Loman could see bawdy grins struggling under the masks they painted on their faces. Apparently so could Taksin. She looked at them sharply, and slowly turned her back. The girls burst into tears, ran, and clung to her long, silent back, crying *meme, meme, mommy, don't be mad at us.* But when she walked away, they lingered around Weyland's outrageous redness, his amused hustler's eyes that told them he knew them, way down, knew what they were really about. Weyland, seeing Loman's face, had grinned and shooed the girls off, waving an imaginary flag of surrender in the air. He had walked over.

"Here's a pimp story for you, barkeep," he had said. "Once I had this asset, a Lao girl, I used her for information but she kept robbing the customers. Finally had to fire her. 'Sometimes,' she said to me 'I jus wan be bad.'" He laughed and repeated the phrase. "You and me, barkeep, we understand that as a kind of basic statement, right? But what about this wigged-out Chiang Mai social worker you've fallen in with here? You think she'd get it?"

"You knew about her."

"Dawee? Sure. Only thing I didn't know was that she was Taksin, not until I saw her here. What can I tell you? Old family, connections right up to the palace in Bangkok and out into the Shan Thern. She was their social conscience. All the other kids go into the family business, politics; she marries military, which is okay, but then gets contaminated by psychology, studies in Georgetown when her husband was in the Washington area, then goes into tarts. Save the Whores, right? The rest of her family, even her husband, figured great, she was their pagoda. But she took it too seriously; she did the lady-eccentric. Campaigns against foreign sex tours, bars, girl sales to the south. Broke too many rice bowls."

Loman had remembered the woman then, though he couldn't connect the picture he recalled of her to Taksin. He had an impression, from television and newspaper pictures, of a tall, elegant lady who always wore traditional Thai dress. That woman was gone; Taksin was what was left, an essence strained through jungle.

"Do you know how Sadong fit in with her?"

Weyland looked at him. "Sadong?"

"Khin's daughter."

"Aye Than," Weyland said.

Aye Than, Loman thought. But he found he still couldn't think of her as anything but Sadong.

"Did Khin know?" he pushed.

"Know what?"

"That she was Taksin's spy?"

Weyland regarded him, his eyes crinkling. "Aha," he said.

"Was that part of your deal with him?" Loman asked casually. "Giving him me as a Judas goat to draw her out?"

"That what went down?" Weyland shook his head. "No, Loman," he said. "Khin wanted me to send someone; you were Mundy's idea because of the MIAs." Weyland took in a breath, let it out slowly. "I could never understand why Khin insisted on doing it this way, having a go-between. But it makes sense." Loman looked at him. What had he expected him to say? He had no way of knowing if Weyland was telling the truth. "Christ on a crutch," Weyland said, "is that what you're on about, an epic of revenge? You going to bring us down for some idea, barkeep? You an idea freak? Hell, I thought better of you."

Loman looked away from him, his eyes sweeping the perimeter of the camp. "I already have brought you down," he said.

Which might show that Weyland wasn't lying, he thought. If he'd been in on the setup with Khin, it would seem they would have somehow been in touch with each other more; he wouldn't have been able to suck Weyland in here. He found he didn't care.

Weyland chuckled. He stood up and stretched, twirling his right hand in a circle that took in the area. "By bringing us here? Let me tell you something, good buddy. You know how Miz Dawee—excuse me, Taksin—got to this place? You remember what happened to her?"

Loman shook his head.

"They were going to bust her, for misappropriation of funds, some silly setup. So she took some of her rehabilitated hookers and hatted out for the jungle, joined up with the hillfolk. I got this today, talking to some of them. Hell, most of her girls were from the hills anyway. I don't know, maybe she was just desperate; she just couldn't let them go back into the bars. Her family had a lot of business with the hill tribes, so did her husband. That poor bastard was probably happier than anyone to see her go. They made arrangements; the tribes took her and her flock in. Loman, let me tell you, the way I see it, she would have been dead in a week without their help. To them the girls were transformed souls and she must have been big Auntie Nat: taking a man's name helped build the legend. See, what the hillpeople did, they helped, but they're poor. They sent all their losers to her; this is a camp founded by losers. Kind of like Australia. That's why she got this crazy mix: all the tribes, Burmese students who ran north. I heard yesterday she even got a Chinese kid from Tiananmen Square, all mixed with her whores."

"The missing," Loman said.

"Losers," Weyland repeated.

"While Khin is a winner."

"We genuinely thought he had information on MIAs. And having any control on Khin is having some control on the trade."

"You don't give a damn about either," Loman said.

"What do you give a damn what I give a damn about, barkeep? You want an opera, you better kill me; you want your ass alive, you better help me out, rely on somebody who knows what he's doing. You say Aye Than was Taksin's spy? Okay, then probably the only thing that held this half-assed fantasy together then was her information on her daddy's moves. Look around. These people are starving; they're already starting to split along tribal lines. The girls are bored shitless with virtue and greenery. The gyre is widening. The center is nuts. You see her lips, Loman? She's eating herself by the inch. Only Khin is going to eat her first. Tell me, barkeep, how did he know where this camp is? That was his big quest in life, last I talked to the guy. You being here was the one thing that surprised me; Khin was supposed to keep you until we arrived. What did he do, let you go to follow you here? Or was that on your own?"

"He released me with his daughter's body. It had some kind of tracking device in it."

Weyland stared at him. A smile twitched his lips. "Sure, I sold them to him, beads and axes for the chief; it was part of the hardware deal. *Kon Ahn Harm Kon Die.* Jesus, I love that guy."

"He fucked his own daughter, used her as a spy, and murdered her to hide both," Loman said. "Your ally."

Weyland shrugged. "Hell, I thought you were in Vietnam."

At the word something else occurred to Loman. "The tracking device? Can that work? All that stuff in Vietnam—a lot of it was just wishful thinking."

Weyland spread his hands, as if to demonstrate helplessness. "Wishful thinking—that what you doing now? You think Khin won't find this place? Sorry, Loman. The technology is much better. You'd be amazed what we learned." He shook his head. "You think I'm some kind of evil character, don't you, barkeep?"

Loman didn't know what to say.

"What I have faith in, Loman, is that ultimately the choice is between tyranny and chaos, unless we admit our power and take charge."

"I thought it was whoring or deprivation."

"People wanna be free, even here. Burma's splitting at the seams. The students and the middle class want democracy and VCRs. The Shans and all the other ethnic groups want to be independent so they can pick on other minorities and do folkdances. Barkeep, the factors are all changing and we can't afford to keep out of it on account of a few old mistakes, old war stories; the stuff losers tell, sitting around on their barstools. It's last-best-hope time, Loman, I truly believe that, and we need to keep a finger in."

"A nat in your pocket."

"At least I know where he is. Khin has the power to be a real player. He ties down troops, he undermines the economy by bringing in goods to sell on the black market, he moves at will with an army on their territory. Hell, Khin's on our side already, fighting an antidemocratic government, though nobody has the balls to back him. Objectively, he's a friend of democracy."

"A real buddy," Loman said. He squinted at Weyland, remembering what he'd said before. "What did you mean, I better help you out? What are you going to do?"

"Get something to eat," Weyland had said.

Now Weyland appeared to be interested in the map Taksin had spread out on the yellow dust. The *Phi Thong Luang* were flitting around her, still whispering. Mundy got up and walked cautiously across the clearing. He stood uncertainly by Weyland, as if he might be of help.

"You think they'll come that way?" Weyland asked in Thai.

Taksin looked up at him, squinting. For the first time, something close to amusement crossed her face. "Do you want to offer your help, Weyland? Strictly in an advisory capacity?"

Weyland shrugged. "I can. I may as well. It's my ass on the line now too, Taksin. You saw to that."

"I don't need advice from your white face."

"Sure." Weyland squatted by the map. "But look." Taksin stared at him in amazement. He traced the lines on the map lightly with his fingertips as if he could see the land through his skin. The two scouts had stopped moving and were looking at Weyland. He spoke to them suddenly in their language, and they nodded. "See, he has to come through here," Weyland nodded back. "The mountains will funnel him."

"This can work," Auntie Soe said to Taksin.

Taksin stared at him, her face twitching.

"Do you hate him more than you love our lives?" Auntie Soe said.

"Do you trust him?"

"I suggested the same move."

"You can trust me to cover my own ass," Weyland said.

"Aung Khin's going to wipe us all out otherwise, do me and the congressperson along with you. You all hunkered down in your fortified camp, just waiting to be hit. Hell, I've already played that silly game. You have to strike first, bring the war to him."

His words reminded Loman of Khin's camp, looking down at it from the ridge. "Khin has helicopters," he said.

Weyland laughed. "I know he has helicopters. I gave them to him. Beads and axes. Only thing is, they didn't come with pilots and crew. That was part of the deal we were still negotiating. You don't believe me? Look up. You see 'em? Why not? I were Khin, I had pilots, I'd be here already. What kind of transport the scouts say Khin is using for his heavy weapons?"

"Mules," Auntie Soe said.

"Mules. Look," he turned back to Taksin. "The way I see it, you got this small, tough, weird little force; you need to use it for something besides filling sandbags, digging holes like you're saving Aung Khin the trouble of digging your graves, right Loman?"

Loman said nothing.

But Auntie Soe nodded. Taksin looked at him furiously. He shrugged. To Loman, the silent gestures and the sexual confusion of their clothing made the pantomime look like an illustration of schizophrenia.

Everything Weyland said was true, he thought, but he could see no reason Taksin wouldn't kill him anyway.

"Fun on the borderline," Weyland said, winking at him, and for a moment Loman was taken by him too, the way the girls had been, by the force of his certainty: he had all the answers while Loman had yet to figure out the questions.

The people around them stirred. They rested their eyes on Weyland and sighed.

"Natives are restless, pal," Weyland said.

Taksin looked around once at the gathering of her people. Their eyes fled hers.

"Hey," Weyland said, "okay, you fucked me, but I'm too smart to be proud. You know what I'm good at, Taksin. So do your folks. And you got a better way of handling the situation as we find it today, send me a sitrep. But do me a favor, do it after the ambush."

A smile tugged at the corners of Taksin's mouth. She covered it with her hand.

That night Loman couldn't sleep. According to the scouts, Khin's force would be there in four days. By tomorrow Taksin and Weyland would set out to intercept and ambush it. "Leave me out of it," Loman had said to her. "I don't do wars."

"You brought this one to us."

He'd been given a mat in one of the houses. He sat up in the darkness. The moonlight came through the thatch, striping the nest of sleepers around him. The air was thick with their breath, their moans, the smells of their bodies. They slept huddled together, heads on each other's shoulders or legs, couched in the trusting postures of the dead. Loman's stomach churned. He got up and went outside, climbed down the ladder.

The night was silent. A sentry went past, on his way to the perimeter: a Shan carrying a Sten gun. Mosquitoes buzzed in Loman's ears. He wandered toward the perimeter, the dark silhouette of the jungle beyond it suddenly a negative of the jungle that had once beckoned him out of other wire, drew him down the road to Hue. He could see a path, a slight sinking of the sand, snaking between sandbag positions. The sentries in them looked at him and turned away. The path skirted the trees. Moving on it in the moonlight he felt weightless, formless, the insect chorus stirring a strange excitement in his chest.

He heard noise from the bush to the left, music, soft laughter. It disturbed him, not in its incongruity, but because it too seemed to have leached into the air from his memory. The laughter grew more raucous; the music was hard rock from a Thai radio station; it was all bar noise.

The path turned in on itself and went into some trees. At its bend was a small bamboo hootch, an ammunition storage area. A hard pattern of light leaked out between the bamboo and stained the jungle with stripes of color, as the moonlight in the house he'd left had painted the skins of the sleepers. He opened the door.

The nakedness of the people inside was blunt; it struck Loman like a blow: the simple, undeniable presence of it like truth under clothing and costumes, the crude utility of genitalia, the smooth innocence of skin broken by the dark, marking thatches of hair, the oily shine of fluids. Mundy was on his back, resting against an ammunition crate, his eyes closed, a girl snuggled on his chest. His face and stomach and soft cock, lying spent on his thigh, were smeared with red and green makeup from the girl's face. Another girl, thin and smooth and brown, lay sleeping to his side, her knees drawn up and clutched to her chest, the heart shape of her buttocks open to Loman, a black, pearled tuft showing, a secret soul pulling him. Weyland and his girl writhed on the floor, the slap of their bodies a purity of need. Weyland raised his makeup smeared face to Loman, his white, fleshy shoulders furred with red hair, his eyes rolling. He pushed himself up with his arms, lifting his sweat-gleamed chest and shoulders.

"Sometimes," he gasped, each word punctuated by a thrust, "I jus wan be bad."

Loman turned away. He started to leave.

"No, barkeep, stay," Weyland called. He stopped, the girl under him muttering in protest. Weyland rolled off her, his stocky body painted as a harlequin, his erection jabbing the air with defiant obscenity, his face a painted leer. He pointed at the girl sleeping next to Mundy. "She's for you, barkeep."

"You bastard," Loman said, but he didn't move, the nakedness of the girl on the floor holding him, the strength of the need confirming him. His life was within the nature of things: he was tired to death of redemption and he didn't even believe in sin.

He moved to loosen his *longyi*, his fingers fumbling at the front knot, the gesture bringing Sadong alive to him again so that he almost wrapped himself again. As he let the garment drop he felt her drop from him also, a coil of sadness and defeat in his stomach that dissolved but even as he understood that he was alone now, still all that mattered was the need, even as he knew it wouldn't be enough, that after the brief, sharp shuddering joining he would come back to himself and wake with his aloneness, the wound of being ripped again from Sadong. Weyland was smiling at him terribly, as if the face of his need had been painted on the air. He felt the air of his naked skin warm and wet as flesh touching him before he touched the skin of the sleepy girl, who had now turned to him with half-lidded eyes, brimming with their own acknowledgment of defeat, bored shitless with virtue and greenery as she reached for him. He sank to her, two MIAs finding each other, two fuck-ups fucking up again. He saw another face pushed against the bamboo reeds, the yellow teeth furiously working the lower lip.

Appetite is everything," Weyland said the next morning. He was cleaning the weapon he had chosen, an M-3 submachine gun. "You ever hunt, congressperson? You want to eat a deer, you figure what the deer wants to eat, you provide it. Teak leaves, laurel leaves, poison ivy, whatever. You're a deer yourself, congressperson, then you figure what the tiger wants. Khin wants to be grand poobah, you give him that, you give him meat, Aussie meat, Jap meat, flesh of his flesh, the dignity of a congressional blessing, even a Judas goat to draw out his enemies so he can kill them."

The rind of Loman's flesh remembered the touch of Sadong's hardening, cold flesh, the hollow inside where she had been. He hadn't taken a weapon.

Mundy squinted, sighting in on a rock with the M-16 he had been given. He wasn't listening to Weyland.

"Lotus leaves," Taksin said softly, coming up, behind him.

"Different tokes for different folks," Weyland nodded, gesturing at Mundy. He was playing with the bolt of the piece, chambering and unchambering a round, licking his lips. Loman moved a little away from him; Mundy looked ready to go over an edge. Weyland squinted at him. "What the fuck do you think you're doing, congressperson?" Loman noticed that he had turned slightly, so his back wasn't to Taksin.

"Come with me, all of you," Taksin said.

"Where's that?" Weyland said casually, shifting the Grease Gun to his right hand. "I don't want to be pushy, but we need to move out soon, Taksin."

"One of our outposts has captured two of Khin's scouts."

They left the perimeter. To the south of the camp was a swamp. They waded in the black, brackish water between the white, splintered towers of dead trees, following the Ghosts. Taksin had taken Auntie Soe, five tribesmen from different groups, and five of her girls, besides the three Americans. The three girls from the ammunition hut were among them. Loman glanced at Weyland, but he just shook his head, refused to comment. The girls had all changed the makeup on their faces, painting tiger stripes of green and black camouflage. The three would not look at the white men.

They went into a forest of palms and banyan trees. The thickness of the trees opened suddenly on a small clearing, formed by the fall of a giant banyan. The root ball that had been torn from the earth loomed up at the other side of the clearing: the banyan had taken two other huge trees in its fall, catching them under its branches as a shot man might catch at smaller men near him as he fell. The root ball must have been sixty feet in diameter. It dwarfed the two captives kneeling in front of it.

The very air seemed stained with green.

Two women in tiger stripes, Taksin's bodyguards, had their

weapons trained on the prisoners. Their hands were clasped behind their heads. Both wore olive fatigues and rubber-tire sandals. They were kids.

One was staring straight ahead, his eyes opaqued. The other boy had his eyes tightly shut and was shaking violently and biting his lips. Both of their faces were touched by the verdigris of the light in the clearing: they might have been moldering copper statues. Loman formed them and their guards into a grouping of grotesque memorial statuary, a representation of this small, stupid war in some distant future. His mind tried to go there, but the sun and the air stayed on his skin and whenever he looked, the two boys were still there.

The face of the first boy wasn't really stoic either, he saw. It was convoluted and bulged, the flesh held rigidly in some inner grip that imitated the ridges and bulges of the fallen tree behind him. A chill ran down his back: he understood suddenly why Auntie Soe had been so insistent about not leaving Sadong's body in the jungle.

Two M-16s and magazine belts were stacked near the two.

"Did they have time to get a message to Khin?" Auntie Soe asked Taksin. "How could they?"

"Does it matter?" she muttered.

"Let me question them," Auntie Soe said. "Come, Taksin. Let's bring them to the camp."

Taksin squatted in front of the boys and stared into their eyes. The flesh rippled in one's cheeks, but the other didn't react. Loman felt a perverse sense of pride at his courage.

Taksin looked up at him and smiled. "Kill them," she said.

Loman spread his hands; he was weaponless.

She seized her lower lip between her teeth and drew the corners of her mouth back. She pointed at Mundy. "Kill them," she said. "Use your rifle."

Mundy shook his head. "Weyland, I don't want to," he said.

Weyland smiled at him.

"Tell her I don't have to," Mundy said.

Two of the Ghosts pushed Mundy forward. One kicked at the back of his knees, forcing him to kneel next to Taksin. He kept his eyes on the ground, like a dejected altar boy.

"Look at them," Taksin said. "Look into their eyes."

"I don't have to," Mundy said, twisting his face away.

Weyland looked embarrassed. "You sorry shit," he said.

A rain started. It beat down hard on the canopy of leaves around the clearing, the three fallen trunks. The caked black mud on the roots began to liquify and drip.

The five girls huddled together, their arms around each other. They were trembling with the boys.

Taksin rose and unsheathed her knife, both in the same motion. The knife was a black GI K-bar. Weyland leaned forward, looking technically interested.

"This is terrible," Mundy said, to nobody in particular. "We should stop this." He looked at the boys and licked his lips.

"Taksin, there's no time to play this," Auntie Soe said.

"There's always time," Taksin said, "for the pwe."

The shaking boy finally broke. He began to hobble away on his knees, going toward the root ball as if it were a sanctuary. Taksin grabbed his hair and yanked back. She came down behind him, her left hand gripping his hair, her right hand and arm across the boy's chest, the knife point in his armpit. The boy shuddered and a fecal smell burst from him. One of the men, a Hmong, said something, and the others laughed hollowly.

Taksin unwrapped her right arm. She reversed the knife and held it out to Mundy.

"Use this," she said.

Mundy looked from Loman to Weyland. "Tell her, Weyland. Explain what I am."

Weyland laughed.

The other boy started to get up. One of the tiger stripes clubbed him down.

Taksin brought the knife back up and let the point rest against the boy's cheek, under his eye. A bubbling moan spilled from his lips and his nose began to run; Loman thought of an animal trying to hide itself with its own secretions.

"You will do it," Taksin whispered to Mundy. "You will do it fast, or I will do it slow."

She dug the point into the boy's cheek, just enough to release a teardrop of blood. "An eye," she said. "Another. Lips. Tongue."

"I'm the chair," Mundy said, his voice high-pitched, "of the House Committee on Drug Interdiction." He looked at the M-16 in his hands in surprise and put it down on the ground quickly.

The boy's moans intensified. Loman realized he was moaning with him, the boy was spilling from his mouth. The boy squirmed away, his terror giving him the strength to break Taksin's grip, but making him too weak to rise. He began hobbling away again. Everyone, even the other boy, was staring at him. Loman picked up Mundy's rifle and he stepped forward and put the barrel against the back of the boy's head and he fired. He stepped forward and out of himself feeling it even as he had felt Sadong leaving him forever the night before. Auntie Soe screamed, knelt, and cut the other boy's throat in the same quick, merciful motion Loman had seen before, a wake of blood boiling up under the blade.

Loman turned the weapon on Mundy, his hands shaking, the boy's moan still coming from his throat, another dead poured into him. Mundy looked into his eyes and slowly raised his hands.

Taksin's laughter mixed with the sound of the rain. The monsoon had started.

4
ZAT
PWE

And the thirty-seven royal nats are called by different names in different times and in different places. And there are countless other nats, just as there are countless souls hovering between existences. The dwellers in the six inferior heavens are sometimes called nats; these are also called devas. There are, as well, nats of the house, of the air, of the village, of rivers and forests and stones and trees, even of activities, such as building or growing rice. Even of the individual. These spirits, kosaung nats, are six good and six bad, six male and six female. They dance between mind and soul. And they are the confusion out of which comes unity.

And there are nats who are the guardian spirits of forests, mountains, and trees. There are nats called yokkazo that dwell within all large, old trees; these are sometimes called thi'pin-saung nats. And there are also those humans who became nats after they suffered violent deaths or were executed; these haunt the place where they were killed.

oman knew where the missing were now; they had gone to trees. They pressed in on all sides of him as he walked. He moved into them, they moved into him; fair was fair.

Taksin's column, two-hundred-odd men and women, boys and girls, Lisu and Lahu, Shan and Hmong, Burmese and Thai, prostitutes and pimp, congressperson and agent, pwe players and Ghosts, went into the green Loman had seen patrols disappear into twenty years before. The deeper they went, the more silent the people became. They followed Weyland; Weyland sharpened by the purity of intent had led them here. He took point; he was the hard focus behind which the others spread out into their purposeless, nebulous shape. Loman could feel the others in the column relaxing into a pattern in Weyland's mind. He fought it in himself, but in the hard rain and the vicious slashing of thorns and tripping vines, he found he needed the certainty of Weyland's will more than the mocking demons of his own doubts to navigate this place.

Mundy walked with Weyland, or rather scurried behind him, as though fear and strangeness had emptied him. He watched Weyland and imitated his moves. His doggishness was embarrassing. He didn't care. "Ruck up," he said to Loman, in dead seriousness. "Laager down." Mundy was humping the boonies.

Only Taksin faded. She said nothing at all, but her silence somehow appeared to become even deeper whenever she looked at Weyland. She hadn't tried to draw him into her scene at the tiree: he wouldn't have hesitated to kill the kid, but Loman wondered if she had also hesitated to test her people that much, offer a choice between herself and Weyland.

On the morning of the second day, the column struggled up a hill that was like all the other hills, a vertical wall thick with roots and vines and dripping underbrush. At the top, they could see miles of jungle, the whole petrified army of trees locked in a silent, strangling conflict under the rain. Loman saw the river, it might have been the Salween, but he wasn't sure. There was a nip in the middle of a great, looping coil of the river, as if an invisible clamp had pinched its flow. On the opposite side was a faint yellow line that butted into the river: the trail Khin would have to follow.

It took them four hours to make their way to it, then only minutes to cross. The water at the pinch ran clear and fast over a clean sand-and-pebble bottom. It was ankle deep. Weyland left twenty-five people as a blocking line on the bank before the rest of the column crossed, then set the other positions in a line along the trail on the other side. When Khin's advance guard got into the river, the top of the line would pivot like a door and swing across the trail, the three sides of Weyland's force pouring fire into the enemy column, the river adding to Khin's difficulty. Weyland had the Ghosts lay booby traps and dig punji pits in the jungle on the open side: Khin's only line of retreat.

He spent the next hours drilling his people, marking the positions they'd have to get into with notches and branches left in the crotches of the trees, having them go back and do it again and again until he was satisfied. His people. Taksin had retreated completely into her Achilles sulk, while Auntie Soe went mother-henning after her.

It was raining hard and growing dark. Loman sat on the bank of the river and smoked a cigarette, cupping his hand over it to keep off the rain. He watched Mundy take off his boots and check his feet, muttering something about immersion foot. Mundy rolled up his trousers and searched his chafed skin, the glow of a cigarette hovering close to his flesh. He was looking for leeches; he seemed disappointed when he didn't find any. From where Loman sat, he could see five of Taksin's girls and three Lahu clustered together, shivering. They were more than cold: doubts were leaking in during the vacuum of the waiting. Weyland appeared and took them with him, one by one, put them into their ambush positions as if he were tucking them in, laying his hand on their cold wet skins as on the flanks of scared animals, until the shivering stopped. Loman, on the bank, saw Taksin staring at him, her painted eyes two bruises on her pale face. It was the face he had seen, a rage held caged behind bamboo, staring into the ammunition hootch.

When Weyland came to get him, Loman shook his head.

"You lost your cherry already, barkeep. What's the point?"

Loman said nothing.

Weyland shrugged and pointed back into the jungle. "Just get out of sight, then," he said. "And don't screw me up."

He threw an M-16 down next to Loman. Loman let it lay.

But when he moved back into the jungle, near Auntie Soe, he took it. Night came. He was cold and tired and no longer knew the point. He lay on his stomach facing the trail in a pocket of jungle. The rough wetness of leaves rasped his neck and face like animal tongues, the rain spattering hard against them, enclosing him in a cocoon of sound. He started to differentiate other sounds in the darkness: the soft, wet scurry of animals and insects, the slithering glide of snakes, the soughing and scraping of trees. He touched a root exposed in the mud next to him, its surface rain-wet and blood-warm, then held it, feeling the pulse of his palm against it. Time thinned and stretched, it was the time of trees.

Until a time came when a lighter but still nebulous shape formed against the oily blackness. It slowly outlined itself in front of his eyes into a leaf, one, then another and another, the jungle creating itself, pulling piece by piece from its seal with him. The washed gray light, silvered with rain, grew stronger. He became aware of Auntie Soe's breathing, the soft rhythm opening an awareness in him of the next person in the line and the next.

The protesting haw of a mule pierced the morning.

He heard a wet rustle of leaves. A faint whisper of human voices. A sound of creaking leather.

The mule hawed again, like a thick man who had finally gotten the joke. A white face suddenly peered at Loman from the crotch of a tree limb, the eyes solemn with the same lingering, unnameable knowledge Loman's night in the jungle had left him. His heart beat wildly against his rib cage. The face chattered at him crossly, focused into the astonished hourglass countenance of a rhesus monkey. It disappeared.

Toktay birds called raucously from the trees.

A pair of broad, callused feet passed Loman's eye level. They were wearing the same rubber-tire sandals the two scouts had worn. Another pair of feet. More. Khin's advance guard seemed relaxed and careless, he could hear them joking to each other. As if they owned the jungle, Loman thought, his own resentment, his sense of glee at being an invisible menace, surprising him. He reached down and took the rifle.

More sandaled feet and now mule legs marched in front of him, all cheered by the toktays as if the birds were spectators at a parade. The line continued forever. Loman counted over seventy mules; when he peered up, he could see each was fully loaded with plastic-covered bundles. The bundles bounced too loosely and easily to contain heavy weapons or ammunition.

Then Loman could only see the slice of dripping green in front of him. Time drew out as long as the caravan itself, pulling him tighter.

The first shots snapped him loose, the firing was all around him and he was free in it. Leaves and vines fell onto his back. A mule screamed over the noise. Loman picked up the rifle and began shooting. Each burst was a long release of pressure. A series of explosions quivered the wet mud under his chest and belly. The booby traps, he thought, and as if there only to confirm his theory, a man staggered backward toward him, holding his face between his hands, blood streaming between his fingers. Loman cut him down with a burst. He saw Mundy, screaming and firing excitedly, having his war. He saw Khin's men come staggering back out of the brush, those still able raising their hands, trying to surrender. But the rope had snapped and the Shans and the Lahu and the Lisu and the Hmongs and the Burmese and Taksin's girls and Loman merged into something that rose and moved in on the surrendering men with the butts of their rifles and their knives and their bare hands, clubbing, stabbing, screaming, a howl of pure monkey relief pouring from their chests. A boy opened his mouth to plead at Loman—his face like that of the boy in the clearing as if he would keep coming back—Loman butt-stroked him, a motion he'd been trained to use years before and never had, but there it was waiting in his muscles and he felt the solid jar of the blow move up his hands and into his arms and chest and if he'd stepped out of himself when he'd killed the first boy, he was now running into what he'd waited thirty years to become. He felt a pain burn in his shoulder and spun around, snarling. Here was someone he knew, a *farang* dressed up in stripes and bracelets to dance before him, drawing his bayonet back, ready to stick him again. Us, Loman screamed to save him the trouble, and he leapt and seized the man's throat, all the dead in him swelling his muscles with strength, and he squeezed until he felt his thumbs push into something hard and it cracked and went soft and the squirming beneath him went slack. So did he.

The others were standing still, looking around dazed, sleepers awakened from a dream. Loman walked along the line of dead men and dead mules. He saw two of Taksin's girls had stripped the pants off a corpse and were busy with their knives, their faces intent on the work. Another mule brayed. The sound rasped on Loman's nerves until he cut it off with a shot.

He walked down the trail to the river. Corpses were floating in the shallow water. One was caught on a spread of roots where the river bank had eroded, as if it had been pulling itself into the tree for sanctuary. Loman's eyes fell on a pair of feet, bare now, the soles thick with calluses. The sight of that cracked, sandpapery carapace of skin, the utter uselessness now of a protection built up over years of friction with the earth, stuck into him like a knife.

He kicked accidentally against the flank of a dead mule, its bundle spilled onto the ground. Taksin appeared from the jungle. Weyland, smiling, came behind her, and Mundy behind him.

Auntie Soe walked up next to Loman. He stared down at the bundle and laughed.

Loman squatted down and worked his fingers inside, pulling out whatever he could get a grip on. He worked out a smaller plastic bag, its contents neatly packed. He split it open and spilled the pastel colors onto the bloody ground. They were bright and false as the colors of poppies. Blue and red and yellow and the traditional white. Taksin knelt and picked up one bright red banner and examined it.

"BVD," she said to Weyland.

All along the line the others were splitting open the bundles, pulling out the underwear, cursing, their faces hardening in recognition.

Taksin picked up another bundle. "Fruit of the Loom," she said to Weyland.

Weyland nodded. "Aung Khin's got a sick sense of humor." He grinned at Loman. "Looks like we ate the bait, barkeep. We better hightail it back to camp."

"It's too late," Taksin said. Weyland stared at her, and Loman wondered if he had heard the same thing. There was the weary resignation of knowledge: the caravan had been a decoy. There should have been mortars, machine guns; the underwear was mockery, a reminder of the caravans Taksin had ambushed. A lure to leave the camp defenseless, for all she knew, Weyland's trick, and yet there was an unmistakable note of triumph in her voice.

Mundy slapped Weyland's back. "Oh, come on, you two. Why the gloom and doom? We kicked their asses."

Taksin turned slowly to look at him. She looked for a long time. Mundy shifted uneasily.

"Turn around," she said finally.

"What?"

She pointed her weapon at him. "Turn around."

"I've had enough of your nonsense," Mundy said. But he turned around. "There," he said, looking over his shoulder at her. "What are you going to do, shoot me in the back?"

She shot him in the ass. He flew forward, his face contorted like a surprised cartoon character. He fell and began scrambling up the direction of the trail. She shot him again, holding a long burst that tore off his left buttock so that Loman could see his spine sticking out like a prehensile tail. She shot at the spine.

"I always wondered at that expression," she said to Weyland, when she was finished.

Weyland grinned terribly. "Know what you mean," he said. He reached down and picked up the pair of red underwear Taksin had dropped. "Would you believe me if I told you I had no idea?" he said to Taksin. "Khin tricked me too."

"Why not?" Taksin said.

Weyland began to laugh and dance, in mincing steps, waving the garment above his head as if it were the flag of triumph. The others had gathered and were staring at him, astonished. He danced around Mundy's corpse. "What d'ye do with a half-assed congressperson, what d'ye do with a half-assed congressperson," he sang. Loman saw smiles start to tug at some lips, as if the battle madness was working its way into people again. Weyland had his charm. He took the pants and draped them over his head like a turban. Taksin slid out her K-bar and stuck it in his stomach and ripped upward. Weyland's hands reached up, groping not for the knife, but toward the pants on his head, as if at the last instant he didn't want to die a clown. He fell over backward and lay still, his red-veined nose sticking obscenely out of the fly of the shorts.

ome with us now, Loman," Taksin said.

"Where to?"

Taksin laughed as if he were trying to make a joke also.

"Why don't you kill me too?" Loman asked.

"I will," Taksin agreed. "I give everybody what they want."

She shouted orders to the people stumbling around Weyland and Mundy's bodies, the corpses of the other men and mules. They obeyed her.

"Take the mules," she said to Auntie Soe.

"They'll slow us down. Khin may already be at the camp."

"Who throws away the booty of war?" she smiled strangely.

The mules didn't hold Taksin's people back. Taksin set her face toward the camp and walked. They followed her, except for the Ghosts, who were too unsophisticated, Loman supposed, to understand the attraction of self-destruction. But everyone else stayed. Taksin might be leading them to their deaths, but, like Weyland, at least she was sure of her destination.

▪ ▪ ▪

They reached the ridge above the camp by first light. The braying of the mules was answered by the barking of the camp's pye dogs, like a dialogue of madness.

On his belly again, Loman pushed aside leaves and looked down at a scene that had been held in time since he'd left. A stand of pyinkado trees, houses on stilts showing above the foliage, a clearing ringed by crumbling sandbag bunkers and scarred by trenches. Children played in the yellow dust. Nothing had been touched.

Aung Khin allowed the illusion as long as it took for the column to get into position on the ridge line. For the members of the audience to take their seats.

Loman drifted, half in dreams, half aware of the buzz of insects in his ear. Mundy and Weyland lay twined together in the root ball of the fallen tree, their mouths open, roots pushing out from their blackened lips. They screamed but he knew they shouldn't be able to scream and for the first few seconds what he heard and saw in the clearing beneath him was part of his dream, their screams edging into the shriek of the mortar rounds, the camp below bursting into orange and yellow blossoms, the ground geysering up into smoke and dust. Strobic flashes seared his eyes. The mortar shells walked into the camp like a methodical giant, then stopped. The clearing erupted with people. Loman heard Auntie Soe screaming something about sweeping around the flank, but Taksin just smiled at Loman, sweeping her hand over the scene below. She had brought them back only for this, he thought, to give him that smile, that gesture, as she'd given Weyland his army, Mundy his war. She pointed the AK at him. He looked away as if he had seen something embarrassing. He was suddenly certain she would not shoot, that she had come to know him, the difference between him and Mundy and Weyland. Her hand twitched; involuntarily he twitched with it, moving slightly to the right just as she fired.

Something cool and light touched his face and body. Its weight suggested to him the shroud that had covered Sadong. The Fruit of the Loom over Weyland's face. He kicked out and thrashed until he was free of it. He felt cool air touching his skin; he was naked. He opened his eyes to a dazzling whiteness that seemed the antithesis of jungle. A young woman dressed in white, her brown face and black hair framed in whiteness, smiled down and pulled the sheet he had thrown off back over him. His skin felt on fire from its touch. The white was fire, he said. "Wiwasfah." The woman laughed softly and adjusted the tube he saw attached to his arm. The spotless white and the gleaming tubes and the glowing dials near his head formed a condition of control and sanctuary. But he felt a fibrous net of creeper in his veins. You couldn't take the jungle out of the boy. External sanctuary was useless. It seemed important to try and tell the woman this new wisdom. "Steralsnatrywholyss," he said. The woman patted his head gently and said something reassuring in a language he couldn't understand but felt he should. Do you speak tree? Her kindness made him weep. She let him go on, patting his arm, speaking long musical sentences in what he gradually recognized as English.

She saw his comprehension. "Mr. Loman?" she said.

He blinked at her, trying to connect the sounds to himself. It kept slipping away, held back by the vines he'd pushed through for an eternity. Like Sadong, like Taksin, he'd been scrapped beyond names.

"Mr. Loman?"

Why not, he thought. You were born, you needed a name.

"Mr. Loman?"

"Yes," he croaked. His voice sounded like a piece of machinery that hadn't been started in years.

She smiled to reward him for his precociousness.

"We found identification on your clothing, but no photographs. Several people had reported you missing; we just were not certain you were you."

He knew what she meant. "Wheremy?"

"Chiang Mai, Mr. Loman," a man's voice said. Loman turned to it, the motion shooting flames down his neck and shoulders. A man in olive-colored fatigues was standing on the other side of the bed. Loman started to laugh: after all his running around, Aung Khin had taken him. He tried to focus the details of the man's appearance. The uniform was Thai army. He was in his fifties; he had the thin kindly face of a university recluse, the type of Thai government official who in his late middle age decided to renounce the world and go to a monastery. Or to the jungle. But the man was no monk. He wore colonel's insignia on his collar.

"You've had a high fever for over a week. Nurse Panchit has been your guardian spirit: she would not let anyone near you. You have several good friends who have been concerned for you. But perhaps it is best if you rest a little longer, before we talk."

"Taknow."

"Excuse me?"

"Said, tak now, 'f you wan'."

"If you wish. Can you tell me where you have been, Mr. Loman?"

"From the Halls of Montezuma to the shores of Jambudipa," he said clearly.

"Sleep, Mr. Loman."

He didn't know how long he slept. A string of impressions stuck to the mess of his consciousness: harsh-tasting medications, the fire poke of needles, the cool spongings of bed baths. Nurse Panchit's blurred oval of a face replaced the darkness, became the sun and the moon to him, in the safe white universe of his room.

Lucidity came back like the unwelcome return of a nag. One day he remembered everything, his fetal stupor suddenly overwhelmed with an onslaught of memories from its past existences. He closed his eyes and tried to push them back down.

Panchit came in and looked at him uneasily and a little sadly, like a mother who realized her child would never be completely hers anymore. She asked him what he wanted to eat and laughed when he told her, but she brought it anyway, though she refused to bring the beer he asked for. She unhooked him from the tubes. The colonel came back while Loman was eating the hot lemon grass soup and prawns. He looked at the bowl and smiled.

"Chili peppers too. You must be stronger, Mr. Loman."

"I'm all right."

"Do you think you have the strength to come with me? There is something I would like to show you."

"Yes."

"Nurse Panchit will get you ready."

Loman shook his head, threw off the cover and started to get up. The room spun. He grabbed the bed railing for support. Panchit and the colonel both stepped forward, but he growled at them. They stopped, taken back by the savagery of the sound in this room where they had come to see him as a child. The sound had startled Loman also. He closed his eyes, gathering strength, then got up again. A blue robe was folded at the end of the bed. He put it on and walked unsteadily across the floor.

"This way," the colonel said.

They walked down a corridor. They were not in a hospital, as Loman had thought, but in some sort of military headquarters. Soldiers, clerks, and secretaries walked around them, a bustle of activity so normal it brought tears to Loman's eyes. The colonel took his arm.

"The Halls of Montezuma," he said, smiling. "Were you a marine, Loman?"

Loman stared at him. "For Christ's sake, who cares?"

The colonel looked hurt. "I care, Mr. Loman. Very much. So do some of your buddies: they have been persistent in reporting you missing."

Then Helicopter Harry had made it back, Loman thought, relieved. He remembered he needed to call Jimmy. But his old life still seemed to be behind an invisible line.

"Ah, here we are."

The colonel had stopped at a closed door. For a minute, he fumbled with his keys, his fingers trembling as if he were opening a box of treasure. He got the door open. Loman came in after him. The office was teak paneled, with a white Pakistani rug on the floor in front of the colonel's desk. A collection of lacquerware and carvings was displayed on shelves on the walls. Loman's eyes brushed over these then were caught by what they were meant to be caught. On the wall behind the colonel's desk was a large teak carving of the Marines' eagle, globe, and anchor emblem. It was lit like a religious object by a soft red overhead light.

"I wanted you to see that," the colonel said. "I took a number of courses in Quantico. Were you ever there? Perhaps for OCS?"

Loman wondered what stories Harry and the others had been giving the Thai authorities. He considered that he was a tree, dreaming the life of a man. But when he looked at the colonel's expression, he didn't have the heart to tell him he had never been officer nor gentlemen nor marine.

"Sure, colonel."

"Ah. Did you know General Cummings?"

"Not intimately."

The colonel laughed politely. "Are you all right? You look very pale."

"Maybe if I could sit down."

"Yes, yes, forgive me." He waved at the leather chair in front of his desk. "Would you like something to drink?"

Loman sank into the chair. "No, thank you. What is your name, colonel?"

"Oh, colonel will do. In this situation, names are quite meaningless, isn't it? Mr. Loman," he said, as if demonstrating how meaningless. "We found you near Chiengrai, after we had received reports of fighting in the Shan hills. You were found wandering in the jungle, ranting about spirits and the missing. One of my lieutenants who speaks English became very excited: he thought you were that legendary creature, an American MIA." He smiled at Loman. "Of course, what you were ranting about showed him you were not," the colonel said. "You were speaking about Aung Khin. About Taksin. About Congressman Mundy. About Arthur Weyland. These are all names that interest us, as you might imagine. I'd like you to tell me what happened."

"Just between us old jarheads, right?"

Something dropped from the colonel's face. "Yes, just between us old marines. Here, in this office. Or downtown in the police station, if you prefer."

"I'm comfortable enough here."

"Good. Then tell me what happened . . . to Taksin," he whispered. "Tell me what happened in the Shans."

Loman was still in the time of trees. Sequence jarred. Looking into a hell to which Taksin had assigned him, he saw the mortars falling again on the camp. His side was burning. He was flowing out of himself, draining with the streams of people running from the camp, breaking against the sieve of the jungle. The stilt house in which he had sat with Taksin collapsed like a man who had had his legs kicked out from under him. The house next to it took a direct hit and exploded into leaves. The shells raked and churned the clearing, resurrected the dead in high, leaping dances. He touched his side and brought back blood. He tasted it to give the scene in front of his eyes a taste. He patted his chest and legs, checking himself. His hand touched the hard shape of the signal in his pocket. He took it out. Harry and his long-gone customers were either dead or draped back on Bangkok barstools with a new war story. He pushed the button anyway. Extract me. The signal was what he had instead of prayer beads. He tossed it away.

He saw Taksin zig-zagging down the hill, waving her rifle like a sword.

She wasn't alone. She was charging with the mules. They bounced down the slope in a brown, hawing flood, the plastic bundles on their backs bursting like flesh, spilling trails of underwear. Taksin's mouth was open, laughing, her cries joining with theirs.

The shelling had stopped again. Loman heard an insistent pulse that grew in volume until it beat against his ears like his heart had edged out of his body. The helicopters came in from the south as if he'd called them with his useless signal, four UH34Ds. They hung over the camp like nightmares, moving inexorably, pouring down machine-gun fire.

A scream rose from the ground as if this was finally too much for it to bear, and the survivors, the people who had stayed huddled under layers of sandbags during the mortar attacks, began to run, streaming out of crushed bunkers and trenches into the jungle, the final flowing of the camp's lifeblood as Loman ebbed on the ridge.

The helicopters darted, strafing.

He saw Taksin's tall thin form run into the center of the clearing, shooting up as she ran. The gunners bracketed her with fire, the earth erupting around her, mules falling, screaming terribly, their barrel bodies, their absurd burdens exploding. Taksin stopped and stood still, her feet planted. The helicopters hovered above her. She raised her rifle and took deliberate aim at one. The gunner cut her down before she got off a round.

The helicopters rose and fell in unison, as if a surge had passed into them from her death. They rose again and began to move toward the perimeter, pouring fire into the dead mules, strafing the survivors, moving toward Loman. A tree near him splintered and he was showered with leaves and branches. A monkey went howling by.

Now he saw the colonel taking notes on a pad, the top of his head framed by the emblem behind him. Loman noticed that his hand was trembling. The colonel looked up at his silence.

"Yes?" he said.

"That's all," Loman said. "I wandered around the jungle. And then you found me."

"I see."

Loman saw the colonel didn't believe him; he hadn't expected him to. He had told what he could, leaving out everything about Weyland and Mundy: he had been looking for MIAs, he had been caught in a drug war. He didn't want to be implicated in the disappearance of a congressperson. Loman understood that in all probability the colonel knew about Mundy also, but he wasn't really pressing the issue. He looked at the eagle, globe, and anchor behind the man again. He was back in a world where if you didn't officially admit reality, it never happened.

The colonel sighed theatrically. "Mr. Loman, you are the remnant of an incident that should never have occurred, aren't you?"

"Semper fi," Loman said.

He saw there were tears in the colonel's eyes. An icy shock of knowledge went through him.

"What was she to you?" he asked the colonel. "What's your name?"

"Names don't matter in situations like this, do they, Mr. Loman. We were together for over thirty years. She hated it so much, the whoring. Can you understand it? I did. I thought I would hate her when she left me, when she took her lost souls and went to the jungle. But instead I loved her more. Is this a sickness in me, Mr. Loman? A sickness in a marine? I tried to help her as best I could, cover her with my troops when it was possible. But she didn't really have a chance, did she? But I didn't hate her, you see. I was proud of her," he said, sitting up stiffly, looking at Loman with defiance.

The man who introduced himself as Victor Demaris was young and bald. He set up a cassette tape recorder on the night stand next to Loman's bed. Except for giving his name, he didn't speak until he'd pressed the RECORD button.

"Are you feeling chipper, Mr. Loman?"

"Chipper? Who the fuck are you—what's your position?"

Demaris smiled to indicate he'd humor the sick man. "I'm a vice-consul, here in Chiang Mai. Are you feeling well enough to talk?"

"I've already told the colonel everything."

He nodded, tapping the tape bay idly with his forefinger, touched the OFF button. "I know you did," he said. "I wish you hadn't. Colonel Dawee was the worst possible pick-up scenario I could have imagined. He had no official status in the case, no right to hold you without notifying us. Nevertheless, I'd like to hear exactly what you told him." He turned the machine back on. "Please start at the beginning."

"What is Arthur Weyland's official status?" Loman asked.

Demaris smiled at Loman, the unspoken word "dead" held behind his teeth. He switched off the machine again.

"Arthur Weyland has no status," he said, telling the truth. "Please start at the beginning," he repeated, and pushed RECORD again. "How did you come to be involved in this incident?"

"I was hired by two filmmakers to help research a documentary on MIAs," Loman said. He told Demaris what he had told the colonel.

"And that's all?" he said, when Loman had finished. He nodded at Loman, as if to coax his answer.

"Yes."

"Fine."

He switched off the recorder.

"Where the fuck is Elliott Mundy?" he asked, but the question was only idly curious.

"Lost," Loman said. "Missing."

"You lose a fucking wallet, Loman. Not a congressman." Demaris left the room.

A monkey went howling by, staring at him in goggle-eyed amazement, as if he had no sense at all. Loman's wound smiled up at him. He pressed its lips together with his fingers and covered it the best he could with a bandage made from clean white BVDs. Other tattered, bloody survivors were wandering near him, staring through him as if he were a ghost. Another series of mortar shells burst nearby but out of sight. Their shock waves moved through the ground under his feet.

The dead were curled in rows of burnt commas on the ground where they had run down the hill, or they lay tangled together in pits or trenches, forming the common sight of the century. The smoking ground, the burst bunkers, the bodies themselves were draped with new underwear, now, as he watched, swirling up in brightly colored funnels, flapping in the wind, the absurd flags of the battle.

The wind was from the helicopters. They landed one on each corner of the clearing as if they wanted to pin the ground itself. Khin's men poured out of the hatches and out of the jungle on the west side of the clearing. They formed two lines. The first began moving methodically over the ground, probing for mines, turning over the bodies lying on their faces as if they were searching for someone. The second line policed up weapons and underwear. Pinching his wound, Loman walked down the hill, following the trail of bundles that marked Taksin's charge. Sadong peered out of his eyes, bright and hard and intent, as if she had just awakened inside him. A soldier shouted at him and raised his rifle. Others turned, startled. Loman ignored them. The soldier stared at him and shrugged, as if to say he didn't shoot the mad. Here and there small groups of survivors, caked as he was with mud and blood, were wandering aimlessly as amnesiacs. A few mortar shells thudded into the jungle on his right, like afterthoughts. The foliage on that side was on fire; a few houses left standing in it were crackling loudly.

A great wind beat down on Loman. It scattered underwear and spent cartridges on the ground and tore at his clothing with angry hands. Dust and small pieces of debris flew into his face. He stumbled backward, feeling the ground open near his feet. When he could squint his eyes open he saw he'd nearly fallen into a waist-high trench. He balanced himself at its lip, feeling dizzy, his side burning. Just above him, a fifth helicopter hovered. It was clean and newly painted; Loman couldn't remember seeing it in the battle. The crew chief peered at him from the cargo door, his machine gun trained, his Asian features framed by the bulbous flight helmet. Loman felt a queasy sense of reversal; he was the ragged, hungry figure looking up from the ground. He planted his feet against the wind, as he had seen Taksin do, and pointed his finger up at the noise and the wind.

"Bang, bang," he said.

The crew chief grinned and fired a casual burst at him. The helicopter swerved, tilting up the cargo door. Dirt exploded to his left, behind him, the rounds chewing the lip of the trench. The helicopter stopped, hovered, and landed across the clearing, in the area already checked for mines by the lines of soldiers. Loman saw Aung Khin jump out of the darkness of the interior. He was wearing sunglasses and his fatigues were pressed and clean. Like his helicopter, he hadn't been in the battle. Walking swiftly, not looking left or right, he went over to the nearest cluster of bodies and began turning them over, one by one. At first he tried to nudge them with his polished boots, but when that didn't do it, he reached down and hauled them over. Soon his uniform wasn't clean. Loman watched him scurrying like a fat olive insect over the battlefield, bending and grabbing. Aung Khin stopped, reached down, and pulled another body up by its hair. Taksin's face looked across the clearing at Loman. Khin let her drop. He took out his pistol and emptied it into Taksin's head. He reloaded and shot again. Then he kicked at the body.

Loman looked away, up, lazily searching the blue. A deep calm filled him, as if his skin had split and he was touching the calm of the sky. He felt himself hum inside like a struck tuning fork, the emitting pulse of the rescue signal caught somewhere in his being. He envisioned Helicopter Harry and his other customers descending from heaven, waving at him frantically from the open hatches as if the men were aiding the machine, the old joke where the airline passengers had to put their arms out of the windows and flap, the mouths of his customers opening and closing at him, pleading silently for the completion of the circle. An end to the *pwe*. Come on. But he stood still in his calmness. No one was getting what they wanted. He wasn't going anywhere. Stacks had to be made. Records kept. Everything had to be accounted for. The heavens remained clear, the rescue beacon, already caught in the creeping tendrils of the jungle, beaming out to the empty sky.

Something insistent whined by his ear. He turned and saw Aung Khin, his face screwed up, one eye closed, holding his pistol hand steady with his other hand as if he were on a firing range. Aung Khin kicked at Taksin's head with each shot. His soldiers were turning to Loman, pointing their weapons. Aung Khin yelled something. The soldiers started running toward Loman. Something grabbed his ankle.

He looked down. A small female nat standing in the trench, clutching him, looking up.

"Quickly, Loman," Auntie Soe hissed. "There's a tunnel."

Loman stepped away. Auntie Soe grabbed his ankle again and tried to pull him away, carry away *Kon Ahn Harm Kon Die*. But there would be no MIAs. He wouldn't leave the dead, the whole crowd clung to him, holding him in place. Bullets whined next to his ears, kicked up dirt at his feet.

Auntie Soe yanked hard on his ankle.

He felt the trench open beneath him like a pit.

He was up on Auntie Soe's strong shoulders, cursing him for taking his job.

The mouth of a tunnel opened before them. They were going into the earth. The walls throbbed with noise. Along the tunnels were enlarged caverns, like aneurysms swollen in veins, each cavern directly under a building or facility on the surface. Each was a mirror image, the same only reversed, under the ground. Under a hospital was a hospital where the dead and wounded nourished and healed the living. Under headquarters were headquarters. Loman, dangling upside down, could see the two levels simultaneously. An American general briefed a room full of reporters, while beneath him, her plastic-covered map the same, only negative, black for white, an enemy general briefed her reporters. The American's face was jowly, his stomach strained against his camouflage shirt. The enemy was skeletal, her flesh only suggested by a green glow, like the glow seen on an X-ray screen, her face a skull. Her fatigues were black side out. When the American's pointer moved right, the enemy general's pointer moved exactly the same, only left. Each move the American general made was negated by the same move made below. The reporters on both levels laughed, but one group was laughing at, the other with. Loman went deeper into the earth, borne on the shoulders of a nat. There are also such things as devas and peta beings, Auntie Soe *informed him. Some are flesh, some are skeletons, some are flesh on fire. They are pecked at by crows and kites and cry loudly. Swords, arrows, and lances pierce them, lumps of iron fall on their head. Those with the eye of nana can see them. Have you seen the deva of trees?*

You bet.

Four of the eleven planes of Kama-Loka, *the sensuous world, are worlds of hell, animals, purgatories, and ghosts that exist beneath the world of humanity,* Auntie Soe *said. You pass through, you get your ticket punched, you start acting like a human being.* Trung *looked down at him from a niche, a tauzang, in the tunnel wall. He was in the posture of* Abaya Mudra. *His gold teeth gleamed. Tranquillity or danger, partner, he said. I were you, I'd get a hat.*

Above Loman's *head, from the world of human beings, he could still hear shots.*

"It's time, Loman," Victor Demaris said.

▪ ▪ ▪

But there were only slices cut into time, opening in memory that would spring into his mind like sudden clearings in the jungle. Time was stained green, the way the air had been stained in the clearing where he had killed Khin's scout. He was in the Thern, the Shan forest, and the Thern was in him.

Ghosts grew around him. He stumbled through them, their gripping fingers twisting his clothing. He caught glimpses in the configurations of their bark, in the muscular bulges of their trunks and limbs, in the pleading gestures of their branches of what was trapped inside. The trees of the Thern whispered insinuatingly to him, attempting to insert their rustling, pulpy words into his brain, smooth its convolutions with their smooth moss. Movement was only the illusion of freedom, they whispered. Up, down, forward, back, sideways, what was the big deal, barkeep? We drink in time itself, they whispered, piss aeons, defecate millennia. Loman was after all tempted to lie down, root. But he kept moving.

He found the missing. He found Mundy in a *saga* tree, Weyland in the strangling vine wrapped around its trunk. He thought he experienced Helicopter Harry and Fat Al and Chuckie's-in-Love as a barroom circle of mushroom stools, telling war stories under a tamarind. On a flat step in the side of a sun-splashed hill he found Sadong and Taksin, Charlene and Usama, swaying together in a field of bright poppies.

The long tunnel he had entered in Taksin's camp twisted through time, led finally to a night when he slept behind a picket of polelike ashok trees, their long, elegant leaves draping over him like the fingers of cold, regal queens. Near morning, lying on his back, he opened his eyes and saw the cupolas above him thicken and breathe with life, as if they had netted his uneasy dreams. He felt something heavy inside himself break loose from the stiff gourd of his body, dissolve and dribble out of the burning wound in his side that was Taksin's last and only kiss. As he pooled out, he felt the filling rustle of leaves enter his veins. The silver light of morning suddenly painted the trees. Loman wept with gratitude; he saw it slowly separate the individuality of the leaves from the mass of night and he saw that what was above him was nothing more than a cloud of bats, hanging from the branches, stirring, feeding on the fruit of the tree. He lay very still, burning with fever and insect bites and scratches, piles of seeds and turd-pellets from the bat feast dropping softly around and upon him.

One of the bats had the face of Victor Demaris.

"Thank you for your cooperation, Mr. Loman," Demaris said. "We'd like to be sure that cooperation will continue."

"In what way?"

"We would appreciate your silence."

Loman laughed.

"What is on the tape we made is the record. Any other knowledge you might think to reveal at a later date," Demaris said, "is of course unofficial and deniable. It does not exist in the sense, let us say, that you exist."

Loman heard a threat in the wording. He said, "I have nothing more to say to anyone."

"Exactly," Demaris said. He handed Loman an envelope. "You'll find a temporary passport in this and a one-way ticket home."

"Home?" Loman said.

"You'll have to reimburse us for that, of course," Victor Demaris said.